isure
cultur& DUNDEE

Mr Spicebag

Mr Spicebag

by

Freddie Alexander

Illustrated by Helen O'Higgins

HarperCollins*Ireland*

HarperCollins*Ireland*
The Watermarque Building
Ringsend Road
Dublin DO4 K7N3
Ireland

a division of
HarperCollins*Publishers*
London Bridge Street
London SE1 9GF
UK

www.harpercollins.co.uk

First published by HarperCollins*Ireland* in 2021
1

A catalogue record for this book is available from the British Library

ISBN 978-0-00-847311-2

Typeset in Adobe Caslon Pro by Palimpsest Book Production Ltd,
Falkirk, Stirlingshire

Printed and Bound in the UK using 100% Renewable Electricity at
CPI Group (UK) Ltd

MIX
Paper from
responsible sources
FSC® C007454

This book is produced from independently certified FSC™ paper
to ensure responsible forest management.

For more information visit: www.harpercollins.co.uk/green

About the Author

Freddie Alexander lives in Dublin with his wife, his son and, he suspects, a large family of mice. Freddie rarely eats spice bags these days, although the same assurances cannot be given for the mice who come and go as they please. *Mr Spicebag* is his first book.

About the Illustrator

Helen O'Higgins is an Irish illustrator and printmaker based in Dublin. *Mr Spicebag* is the first book she has illustrated. It is also her greasiest and most delicious project to date.

To Zelda and Rafe with love

CHAPTER
1

George lived in a small town where everyone was obsessed with Spice Bags. Well, nearly everyone.

You may have heard of a Spice Bag before. You may have even *tried* a Spice Bag.

A *normal* Spice Bag can be crunchy or soggy. It's made up of crispy fries and spicy chicken bits and, depending on where you buy it from or what day of the week it is, perhaps some peppers or onions or chillies. *Normal* Spice Bags are sold in chip shops and Chinese takeaways up and down the country. I think most of you will agree, with the greatest of respect, that most Spice Bags are more or less the same.

But this story is not about a *normal* Spice Bag. Nor is it about a normal boy. No, far from it. Reader, this is a story about the *real* Spice Bag and a rather exceptional 10-year-old boy. Very few people have heard this story. I feel it my duty to share it with you.

The *real* Spice Bag was named after the most widely recognised man in George's town: the impossibly tall and bony Mr Spicebag. People simply could not get enough of the Spice Bag. They ate Spice Bags for breakfast, lunch and dinner every day of the week. It was all that they lived for and, as a result, Mr Spicebag was without a doubt the most worshipped man in town.

So, what was it about the *real* Spice Bag that people craved, you so impatiently ask? Well, that's just it. Nobody knew. I didn't know. And you certainly don't know because you've just started reading this book. But one thing is clear – everybody loved it.

As with many stories, this has a beginning, a middle, and an end. I always prefer to start at the beginning.

It starts with our George, a pleasant and polite boy who lived with his family – his dad, his mum and his older sister, Lucy. George was, how you say, a 'pip-squeak'. A 'runt'. A 'little twerp', if you will. He was as scrawny as he was kind, with fair hair and a freckly nose. He was a decent sort who deserved a decent life. Unfortunately

Chapter 1

for him, however, he lived in a town where the vast majority of people were greedy and nasty. There is no doubt at all in my mind, Reader, that this centred around everyone's obsession with the Spice Bag.

George's town was not always so addicted to Spice Bags, you see. In fact, it had been a very normal town only a few years earlier, much like yours or mine. People jogged, cats purred and dogs pooed (and almost no one cleaned it up!). Nothing out of the ordinary *ever* happened (which, as you will learn, is not necessarily a bad thing).

Following the arrival of Mr Spicebag's chipper, the town turned into a strange one. For a start, it was *always* raining, but there was more to it than that. There was a dark and heavy atmosphere that George could not quite put his finger or toe on. The people skulked from home to work, work to home. The only interruption was the trip to the adored local chipper, Mr Spicebag's.

George's parents were horrible. In fact, it was safe to say that George's parents were the cruellest, nastiest, meanest parents in town. They even had a plaque on their gate to prove it. It read: HERE LIVE GEORGE'S PARENTS – THE CRUELLEST, NASTIEST, MEANEST PARENTS IN TOWN.

After living in the town for just a week, George's parents became *obsessed* with Spice Bags. In no time, it was all they could think about. They would insist on George serving them food (Spice Bags, of course) at any hour, day or night. It was far too often that the poor boy would be turfed from his cosy bed in the middle of the night to fetch more Spice Bags. As a result, the house absolutely *stank* of grease.

His parents were also incredibly lazy and never lifted a finger. They would bark order after order at George as they scoffed down their Spice Bags. It was up to George to wash the floors, and paint the house, and hoover the stairs, and feed the cat, and wash the dog, then wash the cat and feed the dog, all on top of his homework.

But worst of all, George's parents did not even feed him properly. To them, food was a privilege, not a right. They would eat Spice Bag after Spice Bag and the only thing they would allow George to eat was cold, watery porridge.

Chapter 1

It was as if they went out of their way to feed him the most disgusting dish they could think of. More importantly, however, porridge was cheap, which meant they could buy more Spice Bags for themselves. Whatever the reason, their choice of diet for him meant that George was one of the few people in town not addicted to Spice Bags.

George's dad was a judge whose job it was to shout a lot at people. He was extremely good at this job and, because he was so lazy, he often held court in the family's living room, or kitchen, or really wherever he fancied, rather than bother to go to court. Sometimes George's dad would shout at people from the toilet.

During the day, criminals would line up in single file outside whichever room George's dad had chosen, waiting their turn to be shouted at. Some would pass the time playing cards while others enjoyed mass brawls. George's favourite criminal was Fran, an 85-year-old woman, who had taught him how to play the harmonica. Fran had been found guilty of GTA (Gran Theft Apple) on many, many occasions, having been caught robbing an orchard 365 times in the previous year.

Both of George's parents were large . . . very, very, very large. This was due entirely to their complete *obsession* with the Spice Bag. They looked like two people who had taken part (successfully) in an elephant-eating contest after those elephants had taken part in a pizza (-with-extra-cheese) eating tournament.

'What shall we have for breakfast?' George's dad would ask.

'SPICE BAGS, of course,' his mum would reply, and off they would trundle.

Then at lunchtime George's mum would say, 'Oh, I'm starving! What shall we eat?'

'I think a Spice Bag would slide down quite nicely,' his dad would declare. 'Quite nicely indeed . . .' and off they would plod to Mr Spicebag's.

And after a long day of barking orders at George, his dad would say, 'Gosh, I'm feeling rather tired after such a hard day's work, and you know what, I *still* feel hungry.'

'Yes,' George's mum would agree, her belly gurgling enthusiastically. 'Yes, I am famished.'

And, well, you might have guessed what was on the menu. You're getting the hang of it – the Spice Bag!

Sometimes, George would suggest, 'How about something healthy? Some lettuce, maybe?'

Chapter 1

'*Some lettuce, maybe?*' his dad would mimic in a high-pitched voice. '*Oh, my name's George and I'm a spoilt little boy who talks back to his parents!*'

'The amount we do for you,' his mum would add. 'We put a roof over your head, working our fingers to the bone to give you a good life!'

Actually, nothing could be further from the truth. Well, except the roof. Admittedly, their house did have a roof.

'Now out with you and get twelve Spice Bags EACH for your dad and me!' his mum would shout.

'Yes, get going before I eat YOU!' his dad would add before throwing George out the door, much like an Olympic shot-put thrower.

Then there was George's sister, Lucy, who didn't seem to care about anyone or anything. She avoided their parents as best she could, spending the day looking at her phone and blowing bubble gum. George thought that one day Lucy could set up a very successful business blowing huge bubbles and floating people around, a bit like sightseeing by hot air balloon. Someone else would have to give the tours, though, as Lucy hardly ever spoke – she only texted.

George and Lucy used to be great friends, but one day Lucy got a bit taller and a bit meaner and decided that she was too cool to hang around with him. This bothered him at the time but now he was used to it, although he hoped that one day they would be friends again.

Curiously, George's parents hadn't always been so horrible. They used to live in a different town altogether before George's dad had been made a judge. Before the big move, and before their absurd obsession with the Spice Bag, George's parents used to take him and Lucy out on walks by the sea or they would go to the park and play football, and they *always* had time to listen to him. His dad used to tell him funny bedtime stories about penguins flying aeroplanes or horses pretending to be zebras to get into Z-rated films. His mum used to tuck him into bed so tightly that he knew he was safe from rolling onto the (pretend) burning lava floor beneath. However, like Lucy, they had become meaner. This bothered him at the time and it still bothered him if he was being honest. He felt alone and at night he often cried until his pillow felt quite damp.

But life would not always be so lonely for George. Adventure was just over the page . . .

CHAPTER
2

'ET TU, TONY?'

Ms Smith was George's favourite, and only, teacher. She was also one of the only other people in town who was not addicted to Spice Bags because she was a vegetarian. She had wild hair and loved to dress up as the famous people she taught about. Today's lesson was about Julius Caesar. Although she was very kind and enthusiastic, she often got her facts wrong.

'Isn't it *"Et tu, Brute"*, Miss?' asked Cecil. Cecil was the class clever-clogs, a snide and smarmy boy with a greasy face and a greasier personality.

'Cecil, raise your hand if you have a question.'

'Sorry, Miss. Wasn't Julius Caesar stabbed in the back by Brutus?'

Ms Smith was careful not to trip on her toga (made from spare bedsheets) as she climbed down off her desk. She consulted the history book. 'Yes, well, ahem. I was testing you – well done, Cecil.'

The bell *RRRRAAAAAAAAAAAAAAAAANG!*

'OK, class, for homework . . . stay up late because it's Friday!'

George was the only one to cheer with joy. His classmates left the room quietly, slowly, each rustling and munching on their leftover Spice Bags.

'George, can I have word, please?'

'Was my essay on "If I Were Napoleon, What Colour Underpants Would I Wear?" OK, Miss?'

She waited until all the other children had left the room. Then she pulled open a drawer and produced a small bag. 'George, the turnip seeds are in!'

Chapter 2

Now, it may come as a surprise to you, Reader, that in a town with such a gluttonous love of Spice Bags that anyone would have an interest in healthy food. But in actual fact, George was quite green fingered. This did not mean that he was born with an odd and colourful birth defect – no, he was a very talented gardener. He had to be, or else he would have had nothing else to eat but cold, watery porridge. Plus, all the local grocers and the supermarket had stopped selling fruit and vegetables altogether – all anyone wanted to eat was Spice Bags.

George secretly grew an impressive variety of fruit and vegetables at the end of his garden. Cabbage and carrots. Parsnips and strawberries. Beetroot and rhubarb. He even grew garlic. (Tip: if you are ever offered garlic, you should politely accept and stuff it down your socks. It will keep vampires from biting your ankles on the bus.)

Of course, being a child without a job and his own house, he was forced to prepare his meals in his parents' neglected greenhouse, which meant rinsing vegetables with a hose before eating them raw. On the upside, George never had to clean the dishes in his makeshift kitchen, and with all the raw garlic, there was never a vampire in sight.

'Wow, turnip seeds! Where'd you get these, Miss?'

'Online! You can order anything online these days – turnip seeds, or clothes for cats, shoes for cats, cats for cats . . .'

'Cats for cats?' blurted George.

Ms Smith blushed as red as a tomato for cats.

'You're dismissed, George. Have a nice weekend!'

George left the classroom with a rare spring in his step. Gardening for him was one of life's few pleasures. As George pictured what his turnips might look like (spoiler alert: standard in shape and size), life's problems went away. He strolled from the school playground, proudly inspecting his turnip seeds. Maybe things weren't so bad after all . . .

'OI! *WEED!*'

George's stomach turned.

Reader, have you ever known a bully? They can come in all shapes and sizes. This particular bully's name was Karl. Unfortunately for George, he was built like a tank, had fists like saucepans and breath like cow manure. He had a face like a lizard and, George suspected, a brain the size of a Malteser.

Karl saw himself as a mix of a pain enforcer and a comedian.

'How are you today, *WEED*?'

He called George 'weed' because he thought it was terribly funny to make fun of George's scrawny size and his love of gardening.

'My name is George,' replied George through gritted teeth.

'What are you weeding up today, *WEED*?' Karl probed, prodding George's chest with his finger.

George looked at his feet hoping it would somehow turn him invisible.

'What's *this*?' Karl asked, snatching the turnip seeds from George's hand.

'Be careful!'

Karl ripped the top of the packet and poured most of the contents into his mouth before spitting them out onto the road.

'These are horrible. Are you trying to trick me?' Karl stepped forward, grabbing George firmly by the collar. 'Give me your money.'

George froze.

'GIVE ME YOUR MONEY!'

It began to rain again. Karl glanced up at the clouds aggressively (honestly, Reader, he could pick a fight with anyone or anything) and loosened his grip on George's newly torn collar. He had around three tubs of gel in his spiky hair (which made him look even more like a lizard) and was afraid of messing up his reptilian look.

'Tomorrow. You're dead.'

Karl spat at George's feet and walked away.

George's phone buzzed: a text from his dad.

Get 30 Spice Bags on way home or I'll eat you. Dad.

CHAPTER
3

George walked in the rain towards Mr Spicebag's. He inspected his ripped collar. Mum was going to kill him. But he was more concerned about Dad's threat to eat him, so he picked up the pace.

George's parents had a tab at Mr Spicebag's. They were his most loyal customers, you see, and loyalty must always be rewarded. As their waistlines got bigger so did their monthly bills, yet still they ordered more and more Spice Bags. They could not help it.

As he walked past the local playground, no children played. As he passed by the shops and restaurants, no lights shone. As he passed by the salad bar . . . well, no salad bar existed. In fact, the only light he could make out came from the red fluorescent writing at the end of the road which he could not read from here but which he knew spelt 'Mr Spicebag's'.

One of his neighbours, Jasper, a kind and daft boy, would tell George all about what the town used to be like before Mr Spicebag's arrival. The boy had auburn hair, a cheeky grin and a tendency to exaggerate.

'It wasn't like this until Mr Spicebag came along. When I was your age, Georgie, this town was quite a different place. Just imagine, people out chatting and laughing and singing in the sun. It was like a real-life musical. Yes, it was altogether a much healthier, happier place all those years back.'

'All those years back? But, Jasper, you're only two years older than me.'

'Two and a half years. Now, where was I . . . Ah yes, the town used to be full of life, people even smiled occasionally. And everyone loved getting out and about. My grandad used to run three marathons a day. At first, it was just to give his rat some exercise—'

'Exercise a rat!'

'*Please*, Georgie. Yes, three marathons a day. Extra-ordinary man, had to cut down to one a day, I'm afraid . . . never start smoking, Georgie. Anyway, the town was obsessed with straightening up and flying right. That was until Mr Spicebag's opened up.'

'What changed?'

'Oh, not much really. He put up a sign and gave the place a lick of paint, you know. Personally, I would have gone for something a bit brighter—'

'No. No, I mean how did Mr Spicebag's change the town?'

'Oh, right. Well, at first very little. He opened a chip shop, or a *chippUUUur* as the French call it.'

'I don't think they do . . .'

'At first it seemed like a run-of-the-mill chip shop, until one day, Mr Spicebag released his special: *the Spice Bag*, he called it. Well, let me tell you, almost overnight people became OBSESSED. People went from having a weekly chipper to having a Spice Bag not once, not twice, but thrice, even four-ice, or FIVE-rice, or more, every day!

'My parents eat an awful lot of Spice Bags.'

'Yes, the postman told me. Anyway, word spread and soon people were coming from far and wide to try the Spice Bag. Even the President of the United States came to visit. I was talking to him after he ate—'

'Talking to who?'

'To *whom*. The President of the United States.'

'How do you know the President of the United States?!'

'Maybe in a few years I'll tell you, Georgie. Anyway, he said to me, "Jasprrr, that woz thay bast meal I hayve ever had, I bought twenny thousand Spice Bags for ma family and maaay.'"

'Wow!' George said shaking his head. 'Really? Twenty thousand Spice Bags?'

'Yes, twenty thousand. You know why?'

'Why?'

'Because Mr Spicebag wouldn't give out the recipe. Not even to the President of the United States. So poor old Mr President had to buy all those Spice Bags. He still flies back every month to get more.'

'But what's in the Spice Bag, though?'

'Georgie, do you think I'd be standing here talking to you if I knew that? Mr Spicebag never tells anyone his recipe. People have tried to make it themselves, and some think they've come close, but nobody has ever succeeded. All I know is, people can't get enough.'

George continued to Mr Spicebag's. It was now nearly dark. As the rain fell harder, drains overflowed and raindrops bounced like basketballs. George often wondered why he bothered wearing socks. Jasper encouraged flip-flops for the rain, but George lacked the confidence, and the flips-flops.

George considered Mr Spicebag. He knew little about the man, other than his strange appearance. Gangly legs and a wiry frame. A gaunt, bony face in need of a good meal. And a rotting-toothed grin which would turn your stomach. George hadn't known quite what to make of him. He would often observe Mr Spicebag from the queue with the hundreds of other customers.

'Hello, Mrs George's Mum, how are you today?' Mr Spicebag would ask, tossing the food into the boiling hot oil.

'All well, thank you, Mr Spicebag,' beamed George's mum. 'Just the eighteen Spice Bags for now, please.'

And with that, Mr Spicebag would wrap the newspaper around the greasy food and George's mum would be on her way, munching eagerly.

Normally, rain, wind or, well, heavier rain, dozens upon dozens of people would line up outside Mr Spicebag's, edging forward like cattle. But today it was completely deserted. George had never seen it like this before.

On closer inspection, Mr Spicebag's was worn and rundown, tired and cracked, though the red fluorescent lights were impossible to miss and poured onto the wet road out front. They buzzed and flickered above George's head. Apart from some passing car headlights, they were the only lighting around. As he peered in the dirty window, a sign hung inside the door: 'CLOSED – BACK SOON'.

As the rain battered down, George huddled against the door wondering what to do. His parents were serious about their Spice Bags. He imagined the headlines:

'CLEAN AND POLITE BOY DROWNS
WAITING OUTSIDE *CHIPPUUUUR*'
'DROWNED BOY EATEN BY OWN FATHER'
'NASTY FATHER HAS NASTY STOMACH ACHE'

The list went on.

Sheets of rain began to sweep sideways. As George pressed his back against the door, he realised it was unlocked and pushed through the heavy entrance. The room was poorly lit but he could make out the counter and the peeling menus above. He could smell the grease in the air and feel the grit on the cracked tile floor.

Chapter 3

For several minutes, George stared back through the glass onto the road as puddles grew and the odd Spice Bag wrapper flew past. He considered leaving but he re-read his father's text.

Get 30 Spice Bags on way home or I'll eat you. Dad.

First, he cleared his throat to signal his presence. He'd seen this on TV before.

'Ah-he-hem.'

Nothing.

'Ah-he-he-heeem.'

Try again, George.

'Ah-he-he-HE-HEEEEEEM.'

Nada, as the Spanish-speaking Reader might say.

'Excuse me!' he called out.

Not a peep.

George stepped behind the counter.

Now, Reader, I know what you might be thinking. These are not the actions of a polite boy . . . But you have never met George's dad. I met him on one occasion just before his lunch. When I put my hand out in greeting, he nearly took a mouthful of fingers off. It is safe to say that George was DESPERATE.

He inspected the deep-fat fryer and flicked the ON

switch. As the grease began to bubble, George glanced around. A large fridge freezer stood before him. He flung it open and grabbed whatever frozen foods he could find, flinging them into the fryer.

The food HISSSSSSSSSSSSSSSSSSSSSSSSSSSSSSSSS SSSSSSSSSSSSSSSSSSSSSED!

Beads of sweat rolled down George's forehead as he pleaded with the fryer for silence. After what seemed like an age, the light on the fryer flicked from green to red. He pulled the metal basket from the boiling oil, burning his hand in the process. He muffled his roar in case he was heard.

George quickly shovelled the food into a brown paper bag. He had always seen Mr Spicebag shake in a secret spice mix, but the cupboards were bare. He wondered what to do.

George looked out across the counter towards the rain-pelted street. It was dark and the rain was relentless. His reflection stared back at him as the water battered and streamed down the window pane.

As he considered his next move, George noticed a white vase with blue markings not so far from his reflection. Turning to his right, he spotted the vase at the other end of the counter – he had seen this earlier but thought it was a tip jar.

I wonder, thought George as he walked around the counter.

For a moment he inspected the vase only with his eyes. The blue paint was in parts faded but the scene was quite visible. A large dragon flew high above a rural village as the people fled. It was as if the dragon were inspecting . . . no . . . *selecting* its next victim. The artist was so talented that, while the dragon breathed no fire, George could tell its flames were about to torch the town.

As he inspected the vase, now with his hands, he was absolutely, positively, without-a-doubtedly sure that this next bit happened. The lifeless, painted dragon twisted its scowling face. It looked like it was about to say, *How DARE you interrupt* me.

Well, how would you react, Reader? Startled, George dropped the vase. It landed with a thud and CRACKED into shards on the floor.

George stood still for a moment. Had he been heard? After a motionless, soundless minute, he cleared away the broken remains into the bin. Maybe it was a trick of the eye, he thought. After all, the flickering light above needed fixing and could have easily deceived him . . .

As George was about to give up, he heard the faint sound of voices from a backroom. Curiosity got the better of him. He moved slowly behind the counter towards the voices. Further and further he stepped. He felt the floor beneath his feet change from grit to carpet. While the private hallway was poorly lit, he could just about make out a patterned maroon rug that reminded him of his Great Aunt Putrid's house.

A light emanated from the door at the end of the hallway. George held his breath and inched towards the door. With each step towards the light, the voices grew louder.

He heard a raised voice: 'It's not working properly!'

'The problem will look after itself,' replied a calmer voice that George recognised as Mr Spicebag's.

George had his ear to the door. Beside him, he eyed a worn, oak cupboard. He was not sure he had seen it there a moment earlier . . . although it was quite unremarkable and easy to forget.

Yet.

Yet, he felt a pull that he could not easily describe. Like with a room in school that you're never allowed into, he had to see what was inside. He ran his fingers along the front panel. It felt rough and, in parts, was chipped.

He turned a large brass key – which CLICKED!

The conversation beyond the door stopped suddenly. George held his breath, not daring to breathe. His heart beat like a drum in a conga line and he felt sure it would betray him . . .

But after some several moments the conversation picked up again.

'How can you be sure?' argued the voice.

'When have I been wrong?' retorted Mr Spicebag, calmly, confidently.

There was a spew of nasty words that George (thankfully) could not hear and which I (regrettably) cannot repeat in this book.

George sighed with relief. He opened the cupboard door slowly, willing it not to creak. To his delight, dozens of spice jars stood before him.

He wasted no time and began to toss spices into his brown paper bag, willing himself to be quick. One

smelled like fruit, another like wet clothes. One like freshly cut grass, another like burnt toast. One spice reminded him of Christmas; while one gave off a powerful smell of snot (a smell which George did not know even existed). Some spices were flakes and others were like dust. Some shakers seemed empty but when they hit the food colours like yellow and orange and purple would glow. One smelled like his vegetable patch, while another reminded him of a Sunday years before when he was much smaller and his family argued a lot while playing Monopoly, but they were happy.

George was in his element. Like a sorcerer, he felt a strong connection with the spices. He did not know what they were but through raw instinct he continued to throw in a dash or a shake here or there. As each spice went in, the bag weighed more – far more than it should.

'Oh, and one more thing,' added Mr Spicebag.

'Yes.'

'There's a boy outside the door rummaging through the storage cupboard. Fetch him.'

George's gut turned.

CHAPTER
4

Well, let me tell you, Reader. George nearly jumped from his skin.

Like a greyhound at a track (but much, much slower), he scampered down the hallway, through the chipper, and out into the night.

He did not stop to look back.

He ran through the streets with rain-swept wind in his hair, past the playground where no children played, past the shops where no lights shone, and past the salad bar where no salad bar existed.

George ran and he ran and he ran and ran and he RAN.

He ran until Mr Spicebag's was barely a dot of light in the distance.

Chapter 4

His lungs burned and a stitch that felt like a knitting needle piercing his gut forced him to buckle over.

It had stopped raining and the road looked glazed under the streetlamps. It took him several moments to get his bearings. Tall flats and burnt-out cars. Broken glass and nearby police sirens. George could not quite recall how this place felt familiar, but he knew that he was quite a while from home.

He checked his phone:

Missed call Dad.

Missed call Mum.

Missed call Dad.

Missed call Dad.

Missed call Dad.

Text from Mum – *Where's our Spice Bags?*

Text from Dad – *You better have my Spice Bags. Dad.*

Text from Dad – *It's you or the Spice Bags. Get back here. Dad.*

Text from Dad – *Cat's been sick. Hurry back. Dad.*

Thankfully, in all the panic George had remembered the Spice Bag. Or at least, what he'd hoped was a Spice Bag.

He opened the brown paper bag. There were no colours – no yellow or orange or purple. No smells of Christmas or freshly cut grass or even snot. Just a bag of soggy, fried food.

Who had Mr Spicebag been talking to? More importantly, WHAT were in those spices?

Before he could give the matter further thought, a familiar yell came from behind him.

'Oi! WEED!'

Karl, king of the lizards, cycled over with a crew of his scaly-looking friends. They began to circle him, round and around.

Reader, at this particular moment there were several places George would rather have been. Detention. The dentist. Dad's stomach.

'What are you doing here, WEED?' Karl demanded.

'I'm just on my way home—'

'Did I give you permission to walk this way?'

Faster and faster the bikes circled George.

'Please, I'm late. My parents are going to be really mad.'

'Your parents? You mean Waddle-DEE and Waddle-DUM?'

His crew laughed a mean and mocking laugh, and although his parents were horrible, George could not help feeling a pang of anger deep inside.

'Hey, WEED, I'll tell you what! Why don't you share your Spice Bag with me and I MIGHT let you through!'

'It's not mine, it's for my parents.'

Karl SCREECHED the breaks and hopped off the bike.

'Give me that!' Karl snapped, snatching the Spice Bag from George's hands.

'No, DON'T!"

Karl pointed a threatening finger at George, demanding silence. He smiled, pulling out the greasy, soggy, stinking food. 'Still warm,' he said to his friends, who were salivating at the sight of it.

'But, Karl—'

'Shut it, WEED!'

Karl wolfed the Spice Bag down in seconds.

'MMMmmmm,' he rubbed his stomach sarcastically, his mouth full.

He finished up and let out a long, loud, 'BUUUUU UUUUUUUUUUUUUUUUUUUUUUUUUUUUUU UUUUUUUUUUUUUUUUUUUUUUUUUUUUUU

UUUUUUUUUUUUUUUUUUUUUUUUUUUUUU
RRRRRP!'

Car alarms went off.

Karl's friends cried with laughter. George began to walk away defeated, but as he did, Karl wiped his mouth with his great, greedy claw and leapt into George's path.

'Where do you think you're going, WEED?'

'You said I could go home if I gave you my Spice Bag.'

'No, I said I MIGHT let you go.'

'But that's not fair!' cried George, his anger overriding his fear.

'What is it with you, WEED?' demanded Karl, prodding George's chest aggressively. George felt his size once more and cowered.

'You just don't learn, do you?' Karl shouted. 'You do what I say, WHEN. I. SAY!'

Karl suddenly pulled back a clenched fist. George closed his eyes waiting for impact . . .

But . . . nothing.

George opened his eyes, slowly. Karl seemed to have frozen upright, eyes bulging wide. At first it looked as if he was about to get sick. His body made waves as if he was about to vomit. The polite boy that he was, George stood aside.

But then lumps and bumps began to bubble and bobble across Karl's face. His fingers glowed from pink to purple, purple to orange, orange to green. Webbed feet burst from his runners, while his body shuddered and started to shake and quake, and . . . morph . . . into

a dog . . . or was it a hippopotamus? Or a giraffe, or a . . . giraffapotamus! The glow – first blue and green, then purple and pink – was too bright to make out what was happening. George shielded his eyes from the light. Karl let out a loud and strange variety of CHIRPS and SQUEAKS and CLICKS and PEEPS until there was an almighty FLASH of light that for a brief moment lit up the night sky.

Then silence.

As George lowered his hand from his eyes, any remaining fear or anger was replaced with complete shock. Although the lingering smell of Spice Bags was all too familiar, this time the air absolutely stank of the stuff. What seemed like a cloud of steam or mist or smoke – he could not have been sure which – billowed around him, so much so that he could not make out a single, solitary figure.

'Karl?' one of his friends called out.

There was no answer.

As the air slowly cleared, jaws dropped one by one.

George had to pinch himself (again, he had seen this on TV).

Chapter 4

There before them stood a human-sized lizard. Dry, green, scaly skin. Four limbs with sharp, clawed feet. A short neck and swivelling, unblinking eyes. And a long, weak, fatty tail.

George did not know how to put it any other way: Karl was more Karl-like than ever.

'Karl?' asked another of his friends.

Karl whipped out his incredibly long tongue, snatching an insect from the air, and scurried up a nearby tree.

They were all flabbergasted for a brief moment . . . Then . . .

'AAAAAAAAAAAAAAAAAAAAAAAAAAAAAA AAAAAAAAHHHHHHHHH!!!!' screamed one of Karl's larger friends.

The rest of his friends joined in to make up the chorus: 'AHHHHHHHHHHHHHHHHHHHHHHAAA AAaaaaaAAAAAAAAAAAAAAAAAAAAAAAAAA AAAAAAAAAAHHHHHHAaaaaaaaaaaaaaaaaaa . . . AHHHHHHHHHHHHHHHHHHHHHHHHHHHH HHHHHHHHHHHHHHHH!!!!!!!'

Falling over each other, spilling change and phones (not their own), they scarpered into the night.

As George stood dazed, alone, the screams grew fainter

and fainter. Having never experienced such a shocking turn of events, and unable to believe his luck, he simply did not know how to react.

After several moments, he began to shuffle a stunned shuffle in the direction of home.

Just as he thought his evening was coming to an end, George made out headlights floating gracelessly through the darkness. As the car got closer and closer, veering from left to right, it began speeding in his direction.

BEEEEEP! BEEEEEEEEEEEEP!

BEEP-BEEP-BEEP-BEEEEEEEEEEEEEEEEEE EEEEEEEEEEEEEEEP!

BEEEEEEEEEEEEEEEEEEEEEEEEEEEEEEEEE EEEEEEEEEEP!

CHAPTER
5

G eorge had little time to react. As the car veered out of control, he dived just in time. Thankfully, the concrete footpath broke his fall.

The tyres skidded and scrEEEEEEched, and there sounded a large CRASH!

George stood feeling dizzy and dazed. Smoke billowed from the bonnet of a light blue (now retired) Volkswagen Beetle. After a moment's hesitation, he limped over, waving smoke from his path.

The driver's door opened, breaking clean from its hinges. Out slumped a recognisable figure.

'JASPER!'

George joggled (note: a mix between a jog and a hobble) to help his friend who lay on the ground, still like stone.

Light spilled from the split streetlamp. The damp road and glass shards glistened. After some seconds, Jasper opened his eyes, also suffering from a bad dose of dizz and daze. Sitting up slowly and wincing, he looked around muddled and befuddled.

'Georgie? What are you doing here?'

He tried to stand but was somewhat concussed. George gently held him by the shoulders in an upright position.

'Jasper, are you OK?'

Chapter 5

'Don't worry about little old me, Georgie. Sticks and stones will break my bones and all that.'

'Yes, and you were just in a car accident! What were you doing driving around anyway? You're twelve!'

'Flyers,' Jasper coughed and spluttered.

'Excuse me?'

Jasper managed to pull himself up and limped over to the car. He opened the boot to reveal stacks of cardboard boxes.

George picked a flyer from one of the boxes.

'Invitations for my grandad's birthday. At the zoo. He's 115 and—'

George was worried, but this was too much. '115!'

Jasper perked up slightly. 'Yes, a wonderful man! Still does a marathon a day, used to be three – never start smoking, Georgie, terrible habit . . .'

'But what are you doing HERE?'

'I could ask you the very same thing. Why are you strolling around this neck of the woods in the dark? Isn't it your parents' feeding time?'

George did not appreciate his parents being described like animals, but he knew there was no malice in Jasper's words.

And so, he explained the evening's events to his friend who stood listening in awe and disbelief. Jasper forgot all about his head injuries (although this may have been down to the concussion rather than George's storytelling ability).

'. . . and there was something in those spices that turned Karl into a lizard, I just know it!'

Jasper stood grinning vacantly from ear to ear, blood trickling down his face. 'Wow. Georgie, that is . . . INCREDIBLE!'

The outburst startled George.

Jasper danced around, going off on one. 'I mean, sure, I wondered what was going on with this town but . . . spices? LIZARDS? Mad! I thought it was something far duller, like constipation. I honestly thought the town was constipated, what with all the rubbish they eat but this – *this* is BRILLIANT! And Karl, wow! Ho, ho, he got what was coming to him—'

'JASPER!'

'Yes, Georgie?'

'Listen. I think we need to call an ambulance for you. And the police – about Karl.'

Chapter 5

'Oh, Georgie, my boy,' Jasper tutted, placing an arm around George's shoulder. 'This is a matter for the Council.'

'The Council?'

'The Council of the Elder Children. Oh, come on – you haven't heard of the Council?'

George stared blankly. Although he had lived in the town for well over a year, he still felt like an outsider.

'The Council presides over all matters to do with children. They are a group of the wisest children, elected each year by the outgoing leader.'

'Leader?'

'The leader is chosen by the children to lead the Council, and the Council decides on all things to do with children.'

'What? This is ridiculous – how haven't I heard about this before?'

'Maybe you don't get out enough,' considered Jasper. 'Well, except for Mr Spicebag's, of course. Those parents of yours really do love their Spice Bags.'

Jasper smiled sympathetically and clapped George on the back.

'C'mon, Georgie, we have not but a second to lose.'

Jasper stumbled away from the now flaming Volkswagen Beetle. George had to get home, but he was far too intrigued and so he followed. Besides, without the Spice Bag, George's parents would kill him. There was nothing left to lose.

It was getting late. The moon shone brightly and the rain had cleared. The two boys walked in the direction of the forest, which stood in darkness next to their small town. The air was cool and the wind blew the trees so that their leaves could be heard loud and clear.

They walked for what felt like an hour (because it was) as Jasper yammered on enthusiastically about his grandad and his birthday plans. The trees were wide and plentiful as they zigzagged through the forest. After what seemed like an age, George stopped to catch his breath.

'Jasper, how far away are we? It's pitch black. Do you know where you're going?'

'This way!' Jasper beamed, pointing purposefully.

Having lost all faith, George was about to turn back. After all, Reader, it was late and a dark forest was no place for two boys at night, especially with a lizard boy running loose.

It was then that they heard the faint sound of drums. Jasper turned to George and smiled.

CHAPTER
6

The steady beat of the drums was hypnotic and grew louder with each step.

Jasper held back a large branch and George stepped into an open space which was almost completely free of trees. I say *almost*, Reader, for before them stood a solitary, *GIGANTIC* Copper Beech tree. It appeared to be dotted with thousands of candles and, while George wondered what a fire safety inspector might say, its beauty was breath-taking.

As they approached the vast tree, George could see many children immersed in activity. Some pushed wheelbarrows, others carried firewood, while in the distance others dug up vegetables. This was a place like no other, and these children looked like none

George had ever seen. Their hair was long and scraggy; their clothes were muddy and raggy. But there was something else that was different: there was not a Spice Bag in sight.

Suddenly a loud horn sounded. It was dull but over-powering and echoed through the forest. Then came the sound of old pots and pans which the children banged with sticks and rocks: a mark of intimidation. Some children growled, others snarled, and George's curiosity turned to fear. Jasper however seemed unruffled.

A tall, athletic girl about George's age approached them authoritatively.

'State your name and purpose of visit.'

A rather concussed Jasper took the lead. 'Good evening, m'lady Ana,' said Jasper, bowing. 'We seek guidance from the Council. My friend here turned a rather large and ugly child into a rather large and ugly lizard.'

The girl was taken aback by this news, but could not ignore the blood pouring down Jasper's face. 'You need to go to the infirmary.' Ana snapped her fingers. 'Isaac, Hamish!'

A pair of conjoined twins appeared from the crowd. One was tall, the other short. They shared a mouth and spoke as one. 'This way, please,' they said. Jasper wandered off in a daze with the twins.

With that, Ana walked quickly towards the Copper Beech, and George followed because it felt obvious that he should. 'Are you in the Council?' he asked, already out of breath.

'Good one,' laughed Ana, at the base of the great tree. 'What did you say your name was?'

'George.'

'So, this is your first time here, George. C'mon, the Council will be keen to see you.'

As they climbed up and up the great tree, George was blown away by the buzz about the place. The tree itself was intertwined with all sorts of activity: a kitchen with a screaming head chef (a child, of course) demanding plates of fizzy cola salads and popping popcorn (much better than flat popcorn, Reader); an adult crèche where children could leave their parents while they roamed the tree ('But I'm a very important man,' shouted one man in a three-piece suit from the wooded cage. 'You should be doing what I say, not the other way around!'); and an enormous wooden vault with a valve which George inspected curiously.

'What's this?' he asked, opening the latched door to the vault.

'DON'T!' Ana shouted.

But it was too late.

Hundreds, no, THOUSANDS of conkers came firing from the box, bouncing down the tree.

Ana dived and slammed the door shut.

'That's our conker vault. *NOBODY* goes in there without the Council's permission.'

'Sorry, Ana,' George said, ashamed.

Up they climbed until there was no more tree left. They were so high that the branches creaked and swayed, and the breeze had picked up significantly. Pale-faced, George dared not look down.

'George,' interrupted Ana. 'The Council is ready for you.'

CHAPTER
7

George felt nervous. He had no idea what to expect. He was now at the very top of the gigantic tree and could feel the cool night air against his cheeks. The full moon shone brightly and he could see his entire town spread out below him.

To George's great relief, a sturdy, fenced platform with a fine wooden roof extended out over the branches. Seven cloaked figures sat on cushions with candles placed between each of them. This was the Council of the Elder Children, made up of the wisest of all of the children in George's town, elected to provide guidance to those who came before them.

George was unsure who to face, what to do, and what

to say. He considered clearing his throat again like he'd seen on TV.

'Welcome,' exclaimed one of the hoods suddenly, firmly.

It was difficult to make out which one of the Elders was talking because of the flickering candlelight. Slowly, the figure stood to his feet. His hands rose and the hood was drawn back.

George was surprised to see the boy's face was grey and wrinkled. He had a squint, and his hair was white and thinning. He was short (made shorter by his hunched posture) and held a walking stick for support. George found this quite horrifying at first and was relieved to discover that the boy was in fact wearing a very impressive costume. It seemed he took the role of Elder Child very seriously and, to be fair, he certainly had the right aura about him. He appeared wise beyond his years and, though only a little older than George, the boy could easily have passed for a 90-year-old.

Like through a window into his soul, the boy looked deeply into George's eyes and, after several uncomfortable moments, he smiled kindly.

'George, welcome to the Council.' His voice was slightly hoarse. 'My name is Barnaby, Leader of the Elder Children.

'I understand you have had quite an evening,' he continued. 'Can we fetch you something to eat or drink, perhaps?'

'Oh. Erm, no . . . thank you, Mr Barnaby!'

'Just Barnaby.'

'Sorry. Mr Just Barnaby.'

'No, George. I mean, you can call me *Barnaby*.'

George blushed.

Barnaby introduced the other Elder Children one by one.

'This is Wax.' A small, grubby boy pulled back his hood. In fact, the boy was covered in candle wax of various colours – white, green, yellow, and red.

Wax approached George quickly. He looked George up and down. At a guess, George thought he could be about 11 years old.

'George, do you like candles?' he asked.

'Eh, yes. You've done a wonderful job here, Wax. Really.'

'Yeah, well. Just remember, it's my job. The candles I mean. Only I touch the candles. So just in case you had any ideas—'

'He understands,' Barnaby interrupted firmly. 'Sit down, Wax.'

'Next, we have Nerd. She is the smartest child for miles. If you have any problems with your homework, or need any teachers *sorted out*, Nerd can help you.'

A tall, skinny girl about George's age with poor posture scurried over like a squirrel. 'Hello, George. If there's anything I can help you with . . . Pythagoras' theorem or the Battle of Waterloo . . . making a teacher disappear or help with a chemistry project. Anything at all, I'm happy to help.'

'Did you just say "*make a teacher disappear*"?' George asked, puzzled.

'Thank you, Nerd,' smiled Barnaby warmly. 'Next we have Cry Baby. Cry Baby, would you like to meet George?'

The fourth hood came down to reveal a pale, black haired boy with bloodshot eyes. He was rigid and walked over sniffling.

'Hello, Cry Baby,' smiled George, extending his hand.

Cry Baby looked at George's hand, welled up, and let out a long whinge.

'WwwwAAAAAAAAAAAAAAAAHHHHHHH HHHHHHHH—'

Barnaby frowned in frustration, massaging his temples. 'Moving along swiftly, please meet Sweets.'

A portly boy pulled back his hood and ambled forward with a brown paper bag in one hand and a jelly worm in the other. He had very rosy cheeks and considered George calmly while chewing the jelly, a bit like a cow chews grass. He did not say a word and sat back down.

'Atta boy, Sweets!' smiled Barnaby. 'Next we have Heidi. Now where has she gone? Heidi is called *Heidi* because she is the best at hide-and-go-seek. Heidi!'

'Yes, Barnaby?'

George jumped. Heidi stood right beside George, although he had not seen or heard her approach. She was a slight and sprightly nine-year-old with dark brown hair.

'Ah, ha,' Barnaby chuckled. 'Heidi, there you are.'

'Wow! THAT was amazing!' exclaimed George. 'I didn't even see you. How did you get from over there to here without—' But by the time George turned back around Heidi had disappeared again.

'What a talented girl,' Barnaby said. 'Last but not least, we have ADDY!'

A girl bombed around the platform, knocking candles in her stride. Wax scurried behind her, putting out flames carefully with a bucket of water.

'Pleased-ta-meetcha,' Addy said, her hair wild, her legs short and muscular. She grabbed George's hand, nearly dislocating his arm.

'Addy is the youngest of our group, but makes up for it in enthusiasm. Don't you, Addy?'

'You betcha, Barnaby,' Addy replied, before disappearing like a whip.

'So that's the gang. Now, George,' Barnaby said, sitting back down. 'I'm afraid we are very busy. As you may be aware, the Playground Olympics are approaching. If you don't mind, perhaps you might like to regale us with this evening's events.'

And so, George told them all about Mr Spicebag and what he had overheard on his evening's visit. He told them about the spices and their colours, and Karl's satisfying transformation.

'Let me get this straight,' Barnaby said softly, hands clasped together as if praying, eyes closed in concentration. 'Karl . . . is a lizard.'

'Yes.'

Barnaby looked around at his fellow Elders, his poker face unreadable.

'Karl is gone?' blurted Cry Baby. While his respect for Barnaby was unconditional, this news was overwhelming.

With that, all the Elders sprang to their feet and danced, candles aloft. All except for Barnaby who sat stony-faced. Sweets did an incredibly impressive back-flip while Addy ran over to the horn and blew it loudly.

Like Chinese Whispers, news travelled quickly down the tree. Soon cries, yelps, and howls of joy could be heard below. Pots and pans clamoured and fireworks began to explode. Yes, Reader, the celebrations were well and truly getting completely out of hand.

To George, the Council had not grasped the gravity of the situation at all. They were far more excited about Karl's downfall than how it had happened in the first place. He felt deflated and made for the rope ladder. As he was about to leave, Barnaby caught up with him and whispered into his ear.

'Beware of Mr Spicebag and all that he preaches. All his tricks are not what they seem. And while Karl is a vile bully of a child, he is still just that – a child. I have a feeling that you will be seeing a lot more of Mr

Spicebag. We must find Karl. But above all, please be careful. Promise me.'

George parted for home with a now entirely bandaged Jasper, who reminded him of a mummy from Ancient Egypt. Although he took Barnaby's advice, he felt none the wiser. More importantly, he now faced the wrath of his dad's raging stomach.

It was late. Very late. As he turned the corner down his cul-de-sac, the only sound that could be heard was stray cats fighting.

As slowly and as softly as he could, he turned his front door key. Nervously, he avoided the noisy floor-boards in his hallway and made for bed. But as he climbed the stairs carefully, the living room door swung open behind him.

'George, there you are. Come down here.'

George's dad seemed oddly jovial for this hour of the day (or any hour of the day come to think of it). As he entered the room, George's face drained. There in his dad's brown leather armchair next to the fireplace sat that instantly recognisable wiry and spiny frame, legs crossed. That yellow-toothed, greasy grin smiled broadly at George. There sat Mr Spicebag.

CHAPTER
8

George froze. For a moment there was no sound but for the clock on the mantelpiece. It would soon chime midnight.

TICK...TOCK...TICK...TOCK...TICK...

George's parents and Lucy all sat on the old leather couch opposite the fireplace. Lucy blew bubble gum and stared into her phone. George could tell by the glint in her eyes that she found this all very entertaining. The room stank of Spice Bags, which appeared to have a calming effect over George's parents. But it was Mr Spicebag's presence that really placated them.

His parents never entertained guests, but here they sat in their Sunday best: his dad in a grey suit, his mum in her peach dress and matching hat. The dusty, silver

56

tea set saved for special occasions sat on the coffee table while both his parents beamed from ear to ear, staring across at Mr Spicebag. They smiled so hard it looked painful.

TICK ... TOCK ... TICK ... TOCK ... TICK ...
Mr Spicebag smiled at George. George studied Mr Spicebag.

The first thing George inspected were those teeth. Poor, neglected, disgustingly yellow teeth. Teeth that would make the local dentist faint (and this was no ordinary dentist, Reader, oh no, this was a former drill sergeant who had been to war, had seen terrible, terrible things, and made George do press-ups any time he needed a filling).

Mr Spicebag's fingers were thin and bony, a bit like twigs from the great Copper Beech. Those long twigs stirred a cup of milky grey tea (so milky in fact that it was just milk) with a spoon that made a scr*AAAAA*tching, scraaaPing sound.

Mr Spicebag tapped the side of the cup – *TING-TING-TING-TING* – and rested the silver spoon on the saucer. He took a sip and placed it down on a coaster, making George's mum swoon. He rose to his feet, extending up like a wiry lifting crane, higher and higher, taller and taller. George looked up and felt dwarfed. And just as the great crane had risen, a long arm descended. That long twig-like hand, covered in red, blotchy grease burns, extended forward and enveloped George's hand like, well . . . like an envelope.

George found Mr Spicebag's attire intriguing: a worn, dark three-piece suit; a white shirt with black buttons; heavy, weathered boots and a floppy bow tie. He looked a bit like a funeral undertaker.

Mr Spicebag bent down with a nod and a toothy smile. The firelight illuminated his lined, weathered face. His skin was otherwise pale and covered with a film of sweat. George could see that his scruffy hair was thinning. His age was hard to place; he was definitely older than George's parents.

But it was those black, marble eyes that struck George most. It was as if they were independent of the rest of his face. For while his mouth smiled and wrinkles followed, his eyes were vacant, hollow. Like Barnaby did to him, George peered into those eyes like a window into the man's soul and saw . . . emptiness. No twinkle of kindness like in Barnaby's eyes, nor the daftness in Jasper's eyes, not even the glee in Lucy's. Nothing.

'Well, don't just stand there gawping,' snapped his dad, through a gritted fake smile. 'Say hello to Mr Spicebag.'

'Oh, uh, yeah, hi . . .'

'I think what you mean to say is, "*Hello, Mr Spicebag*,"' said his mum.

Mr Spicebag waved away the formalities with his rake-like hands.

'Not at all, Mrs George's mum. Please, he is probably exhausted,' he said, his voice warm and gentle, unlike his eyes. 'After all, it is so late. Where have you been all this time, George?'

When Mr Spicebag spoke to George's mum, he was charming and chatty. Light and breezy. But when he spoke to George, he was intense and sharp.

George was unsure how to respond, so decided to look at his feet (the tried and tested invisibility trick that never worked).

Mr Spicebag turned from George and opened his arms to the room, almost like a conductor to an orchestra. 'George was involved in a little incident at my establishment earlier this evening. Sit, George,' he added, and like a well-trained dog, George wedged in beside his mum and dad.

'Incident? What incident?' George's dad glared at his son in his ever-present, simmering rage.

Chapter 8

Mr Spicebag continued casually, towering from above. Light-heartedly almost, he picked up and inspected ornaments as he slowly paced back and forth.

'You see, George entered my establishment earlier on the false pretence that I was open. It was partly my fault; the door was unlocked. Now, he must have been looking for a menu on the counter. Or a dog, or a toy, or . . . quite frankly, I don't know what he was looking for because, well, I am not a six-year-old boy. Do I *look* like a six-year-old boy?'

'I'm ten,' corrected George.

'Shut it,' George's dad muttered out the side of his mouth. 'You most certainly do not look like a six-year-old boy, Mr Spicebag, sir!'

Mr Spicebag continued speaking in a leisurely way, walking from side to side, as if the rug were his stage and George's family his captivated audience.

'Moving immediately to the point, George saw it fit to break my antique vase, a family heirloom. It's been in the Spicebag family for generations. I got it from my father, and he from his dad. He in turn got it from his old man, and he from his pop, and I'm pretty sure he stole it from his pappy and . . . well, I think you get the idea. It was priceless.'

His dad glared at George. He rose clumsily to his feet and pulled a cheque book from his pocket.

'How much do we owe you?' George's dad said, dabbing his Biro on his tongue. 'Name your price.'

Mr Spicebag considered George's dad. For once it was his dad's turn to be judged. After a brief moment, he took the pen from George's dad and wrote a figure on a spare handkerchief.

Well, this time it was George's dad's turn to swoon, plonking back onto the couch. Flushing bright red, he loosened his collar. He awkwardly shifted, the couch creaking under his weight. Mr Spicebag generously offered his handkerchief, and George's dad generously wiped the sweat from his brow.

'Well, I suppose George *could* work for me part time to pay it off,' suggested Mr Spicebag, as he inspected a chocolate digestive.

'Yes, of course!' agreed a relieved George's dad, 'Absolutely, wonderful idea, George shall work at your . . . establishment. Every day after school. And every Saturday and Sunday for a year!'

'What?' George cried. He had not forgotten Barnaby's warning.

Chapter 8

'QUIET!'

'Splendid!' replied Mr Spicebag, finishing off the biscuit and picking up his coat. 'Well, I must be off. See you tomorrow after school, George. Oh, and I almost forgot . . .'

Mr Spicebag pulled out a large brown paper bag and left it on the table. 'Some Spice Bags, on the house. Don't get up, I'll see myself out.'

George's parents greedily snatched the food up, ignoring Mr Spicebag's departure.

* * *

That night George slept badly. He could not help but think about Karl and the Council of the Elder Children and Mr Spicebag's empty black eyes.

As they walked to school the following day, Lucy could tell he was distracted.

'What's wrong with you?' Lucy asked in between blowing bubbles, glancing from her phone, fingers moving a mile a minute.

After some foot-staring, George filled Lucy in on everything that had happened.

Mr Spicebag

'There's something about Mr Spicebag . . .'

'Look.' Lucy halted, looking George straight in the eye. 'Mum and Dad are going to be really mad if you don't do what Mr Spicebag says. I saw how much that vase is worth. It cost more than our house.'

George found it hard to focus all day long. During his history lesson, he was useless as the iceberg in Ms Smith's re-enactment of *Titanic* (which did not sink and arrived safely on schedule at the far side of the classroom beside the blackboard).

In geography, he got lost and ended up in PE with a different class altogether.

And in PE, he accidentally scored the winning goal for his school when a ball whipped in from a corner hit him in the face and landed top corner. Unfortunately for George however, his headmaster – an angry, little man with high blood pressure called Mr Benson – had bet against his own team with the other school's headmaster.

Mr Benson raged onto the pitch, a Spice Bag in one hand, waving his fist with the other. A vein pulsated on his forehead, which he only got when he was really, really angry (which was very, very often).

'YOOOOOOOUUUU! You are a pimple on the face of this school, boy. Now I have to wear a wedding dress to work every day for the rest of the year, you twerp. DETENTION AFTER SCHOOL!'

'But, sir,' pleaded George as he nursed his face, still numb from the football.

'No buts,' Mr Benson snapped, 'my office after school. Now, thanks to you, I have a dress-fitting appointment.'

At three o'clock, the school bell rrRRRRAAAAAA AAAAAAAAAAAAAAAAAAAAAAAAAAANG!

Rather than heading straight for Mr Spicebag's, George was put to work picking chewing gum from under the desks. As he fought with one particularly stubborn piece, Mr Benson barged into the room. Strangely, however, he was quite cheery.

'George, there you are!'

Mr Benson stood in a long wedding gown, smiling apologetically. He munched greedily on a Spice Bag as he spoke.

'Mmm, up you get, there's a good lad.'

'Sir, I understand the dress . . . but what's with the tiara and bouquet of flowers?'

'Well, in for a penny, in for a pound. Now, George, you didn't tell me you had to work at Mr Spicebag's. If I had known, well, naturally . . .' He chuckled awkwardly. 'Come on, I'll cycle you over. Quickly now.'

And so off they set, Mr Benson cycling down the road in his flowing wedding dress, high heels and stockings, with George mounted on the handlebars holding his bouquet for him. As the two arrived at the familiar red fluorescent lights, the rain beat down hard and fast. George jumped off the bike and approached the door nervously.

'Put in a good word for me, George,' Mr Benson said. 'Grab a Spice Bag or twenty for me, there's a good lad!'

As George approached the chipper, the place looked calm, but when he heaved through that heavy door, it was like a ZOO . . .

It could not have been more different from that night he had been there alone. People wedged and crushed to get to the front. Short people. Tall people. Fat people. Skinny people. Old people. Young people. Everyone looked tired with great, big greasy bags under their eyes. All greedy, unhealthy people with pasty faces and oily hair, waving cash, demanding Spice Bags as if their lives depended on it. Mr

Spicebag stood at the front effortlessly attending to the heaving crowd. The smell of spice was intense and the noise was immense as the crowd all shouted at once to make their order.

'Mrs Murphy, how many Spice Bags today? The usual: twenty-two? Of course. Mr Collins, back so soon – seven more. Mr Sheridan – twelve each for you and Mrs Sheridan? Absolutely.'

This went on for some time as George struggled through the sea of people.

'George, there you are,' called Mr Spicebag eventually.

A long arm extended over the counter and plucked the boy from the noisy crowd, placing him down alongside him. Mr. Spicebag was stronger than his skinny arms suggested. The grease king continued to multitask – pulling up a freshly cooked batch from the fryer, sprinkling a dash of his secret spice mix here or there, while also working the till.

Mr Spicebag turned to George abruptly, taking off his greasy apron and placing it over George's head.

'Right, George. I've to take care of a bit of business downstairs. I need you to man the front.'

George looked rather alarmed.

'What? I don't know what to do. There must be a hundred people in here. I don't know how anything works!'

'You seemed to know exactly how everything worked when you were here the other night,' said Mr Spicebag, coldly.

And while the room was full of hysterical people shouting, for a moment it seemed like it was just the two of them. The instructions were clear. Cook and feed until there were no more people to serve. Mr Spicebag turned and walked away, and the volume was turned right back up.

The people shouted and snatched at George.

'FIVE Spice Bags!' shouted Mrs Oates, the lollipop lady, trying to put some crumpled notes into George's hand.

'TEN Spice Bags, boy!' yelled Mr Butler the bank manager, waving his credit card.

'FIFTY Spice Bags!' roared Ms Burke, a local politician, thrusting forward a large brown envelope weighed down with cash.

George did as he was told. He battered the food, he fried the food, he spiced the food. Over and over and over. Batter. Fry. Spice.

Mr Spicebag

The people came in their droves. And my word, it got hot in there. Can you imagine it? Cooking food in boiling oil in a small room with hundreds of people shouting and banging and crushing and sweating. It got so hot in there that George thought he was seeing things in the twisting shadows – a donkey, a badger, and a snake – as they danced on the wall, though they were (they MUST have been) Mrs Oates's, Mr Butler's, and Ms Burke's shadows.

However, it was not just the heat that George felt caused these illusions. The scent of spices was so over-powering that the room felt empty of oxygen – it was as if he was inhaling a toxic gas. George thought he could pass out at any moment.

But Lucy had warned him to do what Mr Spicebag had said, and so he continued working.

Batter. Fry. Spice.

BATTER.

FRY.

SPICE.

And the people kept coming in their droves. For what seemed like an age, they heaved against the counter demanding, begging, praying, *pleading* for the fried food.

Chapter 8

George's face boiled like a fever. His hair was saturated with sweat and his eyes fizzed as shapes blurred and warped before him.

Dr Charlton, the doctor, barked his order at George, his savage jaw foaming as he snapped violently.

Mrs Samson, the hairdresser, stomped her feet and whined loudly across the counter, her large choppers merely inches from George's face.

Old Mrs Talbot slammed her walking stick ferociously against the counter, baring her sharp fangs at anyone skipping the queue.

And through the wild mirage, George was almost certain that he saw a curly tail on Mr Parson's rear end as the local baker squeezed out towards the exit. He could be heard squealing loudly and George suspected he may not have made it out of the chipper with his Spice Bags intact.

Just as George was about to collapse with exhaustion . . .

It stopped.

The very last person scurried away with the very last Spice Bag. All that was left was a bare freezer and a barley standing George.

He gulped down several glasses of water. In fact, Reader, I think it would be a good time for us all to have a glass of water – please, go now, it's important that we all stay hydrated as there is little opportunity to do so in this book. I won't be writing about anything for the next ten seconds other than George's Great Aunt Putrid's blouse collection, so you might as well have a sip.

George's Great Aunt Putrid owned quite a selection of blouses, the first of which she bought in 1926 in the Irish county of Kilkenny. It was lime in colour and scent.

OK, ready to continue? Excellent!

George was absolutely shattered. But while he was ready for home, he remembered what Lucy had said, and wanted to get Mr Spicebag's permission to leave. For the second time, he stepped from sticky chipper floor to maroon patterned carpet.

'Mr Spicebag?'

No response.

George walked down the narrow hallway. He stood outside the door like he had done the night before when he had heard the voices.

TAP-TAP-TAP

There was no answer for several moments, which

George was quite pleased about and felt it reasonable to say, at a later stage, if required, that he had tried and tried and *tried* to find Mr Spicebag but, alas, he was nowhere to be found. He began to tiptoe away.

'Yes?'

George grimaced.

'Mr Spicebag, sir. I was just going to head off now!'

'Ah, George. Come in!'

Stepping through the door, George let out a gasp of surprise. For what was before him was not the usual basement scene. No washing machine, or Christmas decorations, or boxes of clutter. No. Not at all. Nothing of the sort.

For what was before him was at least a hundred steps down a stone stairway. He scratched his head, trying to figure out how this room could fit under the little chipper. But before his brain could connect the dots, he caught sight of Mr Spicebag at the bottom of the stairs standing next to a large cage. And in that cage? Dry, green, scaly skin. Four limbs with sharp, clawed feet. A short neck and swivelling eyeballs. And a long, weak, fatty tail. In that cage stood Karl. More Karl-like than ever.

CHAPTER
9

It was as if George had stepped back in time, perhaps into a different world altogether.

There were tall, old shelves filled with different coloured books, long oak tables with strange apparatus, and a large roaring fire nearly the height of Mr Spicebag himself. The room smelled not like grease, but like an old library, and although the steps, floor, and walls were made of stone, it felt cosy.

'By all means, George. Please, do take your time.'

George scurried down as quickly as he could.

Mr Spicebag took notes before walking across the room to a large, red book resting on a pedestal. He flicked through a page or three or six, muttering a few inaudible words to himself.

Chapter 9

George stood patiently, politely (because he really was a decent lad), looking from Karl to Mr Spicebag, Mr Spicebag to Karl. Mr Spicebag hurried between this and that, pulling a few jars of various shapes and sizes from a line of old oak cupboards and returning to the long table. He sat on a stool with his back to George, and began grinding spices in a very large wooden pestle and mortar.

Almost immediately, the smells again hit George's nostrils quick and fast, wave after wave.

First the scent of warm cinnamon rolls. Delicious. Next the smell of sheep dung. Not so delicious. After that, he smelled the sound, yes, the *SOUND* of a helicopter right above. He looked up, perplexed, at the wooden chandelier. George's curiosity got the better of him and he craned his neck for a better view. He was sure he could spot different colours emanate from the mortar, but Mr Spicebag was blocking his view. The scents bombarded his nostrils over and over, again and again.

Next, the scent of hot chocolate burning on a stove.

'Well, are you going to just stand there?' Mr Spicebag asked without turning around.

'Excuse me?'

'Hot chocolate. Burning. Stove. Bring me a cup.'

George hastily did as he was told. He presented the hot chocolate to Mr Spicebag, who immediately spat the burnt contents to the floor.

'Well?' asked Mr Spice Bag.

'Excuse me?' asked our polite hero.

Mr Spicebag rose to his feet, towering above George. 'How did you do it?'

'Do what, the hot chocolate? It was there on the stove and—'

'Not that, you imbecile. Karl. How did you change him?'

'I don't know.'

Chapter 9

'You do know. You're lying. You *stole* spices from one of my cupboards. I need to know how you did this. And I need to know *now*.'

'I–I–I don't know.'

'YOU DO KNOW!' snapped Mr Spicebag, and for a split second he looked shocked by his loss of control.

George stood frozen, terrified. The room was silent but for the crackling of the fire. Mr Spicebag composed himself and stroked his chin thoughtfully. It was clear that George had no idea what he was talking about.

'George, how did this happen?' he asked more calmly. 'What spices did you put in?'

'I don't know, I swear!' cried George. 'All I know is that I threw some of your spices from the cupboard on to my parents' dinner and Karl ate it and he turned into . . .THAT!'

Mr Spicebag sat down and rubbed his brow wearily. 'Imagine this,' he pointed at Karl eventually, '*this*, happened to you. Imagine how worried your parents would be, wondering where you'd gotten to.'

'I don't think my parents would mind too much, to be honest with you. Sometimes I think all they care about are Spice Bags.' George's grim reality, his life

77

outside the last day, away from Karl or the Council or Mr Spicebag, all came drifting back into his head. He tried to hold back his tears.

'You know, we're not too different, you and I,' Mr Spicebag said. 'I remember when I was your age, I had parents like yours. Parents who . . . thought a lot more about themselves than about me. More about their welfare than mine. I know what it's like to feel alone, George. Particularly at night when distractions are rare and you're left alone with your innermost thoughts. Eating at you. Night after night. I *know* what it's like.'

The two sat for a number of moments, George staring at his feet, Mr Spicebag at his cup.

'Do you think the spices did this?' sniffed George, pointing at Karl.

'There is no doubt in my mind,' replied Mr Spicebag earnestly. 'The power of spices cannot be understated, George. Harnessed in the right way, they can help you do anything your heart desires.'

'Can you turn Karl back?'

'That depends – with your help to find the recipe you used . . . maybe.'

George nodded, thoughtfully.

Chapter 9

'You know, I know that my hot chocolate doesn't taste like chocolate,' said Mr Spicebag, and with that George snorted a happy, snotty laugh like sometimes you do after you've just been crying, '*BUT* . . . it is hot. And hot chocolate always makes me feel better.'

Mr Spicebag walked to the stove and returned with a mug of burnt hot chocolate for George and a refill for himself.

'How about it, George, will you work with me? For Karl's sake?'

George looked up at Mr Spicebag and clinked his cup.

'Yes,' smiled George.

And you know what, Reader. The hot chocolate didn't taste that bad.

CHAPTER
10

To George's surprise, they got to work there and then.

'Now then, there are a few things you need to know,' Mr Spicebag said, rising to his feet. 'First off, what you did the other night is rare. Very rare indeed. Even I have trouble doing what you did.'

Mr Spicebag reflected on this for a moment before continuing. 'Right, give me a hand clearing some space, please.'

George helped Mr Spicebag push the long tables to one side of the room.

'Plenty of room. Very important. Next . . .'

Next, Mr Spicebag opened the cupboards along the wall. Each was packed with glass jars and containers of various shapes and colours. *There must be around ten thousand spices in there*, thought George.

'Must be around ten thousand spices in here,' muttered Mr Spicebag. 'Now, over here, please!'

The two stood side by side facing the cupboards.

For a moment, nothing was said. The fire spat while Karl paced and clawed in his cage. Then with a start, Mr Spicebag clapped his hands making George jump.

'You are an exception, George, and you should beware of others exploiting your gift. You can tell no one about what goes on in here, is that clear?'

George stared into those black, marble eyes and nodded.

'What do you know about spices?'

George considered the question.

'Not much. Ms Smith told us spices come from our belly buttons.'

Mr Spicebag, for the first time in a long time, was speechless.

'From our belly buttons . . .' he muttered to himself, glancing down at his own belly button, rethinking his assessment of George.

An uncomfortable moment passed before Mr Spicebag spoke.

'Well, George. A spice can be a seed, or fruit, or root, or bark. They were for a time one of the most important things in the world. Even more important than money. But for our purposes right now, to do what you did, it's about how they are combined. There are *three steps* to combining spices.'

Mr Spicebag circled the room as he spoke. He stopped at the fire and prodded it with an iron poker.

'NUMBER ONE!' he said with an abrupt swivel, hot poker in the air, making George jump again.

'SCENT,' he said, inhaling deeply through his long, bony beak. 'Let your nose be your guide. What can you smell, George?'

George faced the cupboards and sniffed it all in.

'Burning.'

Mr Spicebag threw out the remainder of the burning hot chocolate.

'What else?'

'I smell . . . chlorine, like in a swimming pool.'

'That is in fact the smell of ground jigglethorns. Very good, what else?'

'Fried bacon,' George said, eyes closed to focus his snout.

'That's plop-seed extract. Next!'

'Fish.'

'Rotting pinkle root. Keep going.'

'Wet paint . . . peppermint . . . *horse* manure?'

'Glibbersnap dust, ground shnopper leaves, and gloo-penflower spice. Excellent work, George – don't stop!'

And as George sniffed, and called out smells, eyes still closed, Mr Spicebag began to forage through the cupboards. It was almost as if George was a head chef directing his assistant.

'Tomato sauce . . .'

'Ground brittlenector vine,' translated Mr Spicebag.

'Vomit . . .'

'Feetrat seeds.'

'Burning incense . . .'

'Burnt copplesmack extract! OK, stop! Come over here, George.'

George followed Mr Spicebag over to one of the long tables.

'Now,' whispered Mr Spicebag, as he carefully opened each jar, 'after scent, the second thing to know about spices is: they are SHY.'

'Shy?'

'Shy. That's why I opened all the cupboards – so they would get used to your voice.'

Mr Spicebag took out a dash and a flake of this, and a teaspoon or a pinch of that, and placed them all into the large mortar.

'Now, take this,' Mr Spicebag said handing George the pestle. 'Slowly mix the spices, and talk to them. But not too loudly – you don't want to frighten them.'

'Talk to them? But . . . what do I say?'

'Anything.'

George took a deep breath. 'Em, hello spices. My name is George . . .'

'Softer, George. I find muttering more fruitful.'

And so, George muttered, soft mutterings so as not to scare the precious spices. He spoke for several minutes about his day, of his likes and dislikes, his dreams and ambitions, turning and stirring the mix methodically. And when the spices had practically turned to dust, a strange thing happened.

George could have sworn that he heard squeaky rambling (imagine what, say, a grasshopper might sound like if it spoke to you, Reader). He glanced up at Mr Spicebag who was staring at the spices.

Chapter 10

'That's it, focus, George. Keep talking and mixing.'

And as he spoke, the spices began to swirl around in the mortar like a tiny, contained twister. Round and round – they reminded George of sand on the beach on a windy day. Then black, purple, and amber sparks began to fly and then swirl. A fiery heat blazed, George pulled his hands away with a start. A burning, almost sour scent pricked his nostrils.

George blew on his flamed fingers and peered into the mix. The spices had returned to their lifeless, limp state.

'Now, listen very carefully, George,' Mr Spicebag said, barely whispering. 'The final step, after smelling the spices, after talking to the spices, is *willing* the spices. You must have your desired outcome at heart and in mind. Without *desire*, it doesn't work. That's why I think when you fed Karl, nay – when Karl fed himself – it must have been your fear or your anger that delivered your innermost desire: to be rid of him.'

Mr Spicebag hesitated only briefly. 'I think we should test this out,' he said, smiling at George.

'On me?'

'No, of course not. I don't want Child Services in here.'

Peering around the room, Mr Spicebag slowly picked up a wooden box at the foot of the table.

'That one will do,' and with a swing of his skinny arm, he flung the box intently across the room.

BANG!

Mr Spicebag returned a moment later holding a mouse by the tail.

'Beautiful creature, the field mouse. Terrible eyesight though – didn't see me coming, did you? Now, take that spoon and serve the little fellow just the tiniest portion. And, George, remember, you must *desire* your outcome. *Will* the mouse to become human.'

'Will it hurt him?'

'Gosh, no. Mice love spices.'

After some hesitation, George carefully collected the tiniest portion and placed it to the mouse's mouth. The mouse *sniff-sniff-sniffed* and gobbled it up without a fuss. Mr Spicebag placed the mouse back into the box.

'Now, if I am correct in my thinking, if your mix turned a boy into a lizard, well then this should turn our little friend here into something much more human. I call it *the opposite effect*.'

George thought Mr Spicebag had come down with

the raving lunatic effect. The two watched the rodent sniff around the small box. George could hear Karl make raspy clicking sounds from the cage, which he could only assume was normal for a lizard boy. The mouse looked calm and content, and George began to doubt their spice mix.

But then *veeery* slowly, the tiny field mouse began to glow. At first, it was a dim light but then, as if someone was turning a valve ever so gradually, the mouse grew brighter. And brighter and brighter. It became so bright, in fact, that George was worried the mouse might burst into flames. Suddenly, there was a blinding *FLASH* that forced the two to shield their eyes.

And again, much like with Karl's transformation, some kind of steam or smoke or mist filled the room. As it cleared, George was a little disappointed that the tiny mouse was still a tiny mouse.

Mr Spicebag wiped his brow and slumped down at the table in frustration. George peered at the mouse who sniffed around the inside of the upturned box curiously. And then George too took a moment to rest on a nearby stool.

'I'm 'ungry.'

'Well there's not much down here to eat,' Mr Spicebag said, looking into the fire.

George lifted his head.

'I'm not hungry,' replied George. 'I didn't say that.'

George and Mr Spicebag glanced at one another before darting back to the box. The field mouse stood on his hind legs, rubbing his paws together.

'Eh, wot ees dere for, 'ow you say, eating?' the mouse spoke in a thick French accent.

'You can talk!' exclaimed George.

'*Oui*, of course. Reelly zo, I am, ugh, 'ow you say, starving.'

Mr Spicebag darted to the cupboards (really just one large step) and returned with a handful of walnuts, dropping them into the box.

'Ah, zis is *parfait*, perfect.'

'I've never met a talking mouse before!'

'Well, 'av you ever tried to make zee *small talk* with a mouse?'

'Eh, well, no. I suppose I haven't.'

After a few seconds, the mouse was full and sat in a happy slump.

'Now *zat* is what I call *fine dining*. Nearly bettur zen insects.'

The mouse rubbed his belly and began to sing contentedly. In fact, he had a sweet tenor voice that really carried quite beautifully.

'You've got a nice voice.'

'You've got a, 'ow you say, vury big 'ead.'

George laughed in disbelief.

'Hey, do you have a name?'

'Well, not reelly. Aldough, when I do meet, ugh, ze people, zey like to call me *AHHHHHHHHHHHHH-HHHHHHHHHHHH MOUSE!*'

George guffawed. 'Well, you can talk now, so you need a name. How about Maurice? It sounds a bit like *more*, as in "more walnuts".'

The mouse was touched and stood on his hind legs.

'Bah, *oui*! Yes! Maurice. It's *parfait*! And you, what ees yurr name, little boy?'

'I'm George—'

'Enough of the pleasantries,' snapped Mr Spicebag. 'I want answers, mouse! Do you feel any differently than before you ate that spice mix? Any other side effects?'

89

Maurice rubbed and focused his eyes on Mr Spicebag (because mice really do have poor vision, Reader).

'Wait, 'ang on. I know you, Skinny. Where ees your friend?'

'Quiet you!' demanded Mr Spicebag.

'You know, Ggeorge, zis man is up to all tricks in 'ere. 'Ow you say, ee 'as *big plans*—'

'I said SILENCE!' barked Mr Spicebag, slamming a lid on the box abruptly so that all that could be heard were Maurice's muffled shouts.

'Em . . . I'd like to study him, George. If you don't mind, I think we should call it a night.'

'What did he mean *big plans*? You're not going to hurt him, are you?'

Mr Spicebag judged George for a number of moments.

'Of course not! You know mice – always paranoid! You put in a very good evening's work, and I think you deserve a reward.'

Mr Spicebag produced a small brown-leather satchel from his pocket.

'These are very . . . *special*,' explained Mr Spicebag. 'They're called golly-squash seeds.'

'Golly-squash seeds?'

Chapter 10

'I suggest you try some before the Playground Olympics.'

George did not recall having told him about the Playground Olympics.

'Now, home with you. We're closed.'

CHAPTER
11

'George, bring us some more Spice Bags!' shouted George's dad.

George's parents always made sure that they were well stocked with leftovers for breakfast until Mr Spicebag's opened for business.

George returned to the kitchen table with six Spice Bags. His parents made light work of the defenceless leftovers. As usual, Lucy sat silently blowing bubble gum and texting.

'Did 'oo wash the dog?' asked his mum, mouth full.

'Yes, mum,' replied George as he pushed his watery porridge around his bowl.

'Wha' abou' the ca'?' chewed his dad, spitting bits of food onto George's cat-scratched face.

'Yes, dad.'

'An' di' 'ou 'oover du stairs?' quizzed his mum, ripping open another Spice Bag.

'Yes, mum.'

'An' the woof?' George's dad demanded before swallowing. 'Did you fix the roof?'

'No, I got back late from Mr Spicebag's last night and it was raining. I'll do it after—'

George's dad slammed the table with the palm of his hand. 'Do you know, I do not care for this attitude of yours!' George looked into his bowl. 'Don't you ignore me, boy! Do you take your mother and me for fools?!'

'No, Dad. I'm sorry, Dad.'

'Oh, no, Dad. Oh, I'm sorry, Dad. Oh, I take everything for granted because I'm a spoilt little boy, Dad!' his dad mimicked cruelly in a high-pitched tone, waving his fingers sarcastically.

'Now,' he said, grabbing George's porridge. 'Take this . . . *filth*, and FIX. MY. ROOF!'

George clambered on to the roof with his porridge. Raindrops began to puddle in his breakfast. The roof slates were damp and the rain seeped through his trousers to his bottom when he sat down to work.

He had slept poorly the night before, having found it hard to get Maurice out of his mind. He took the small leather satchel from his pocket and inspected the golly-squash seeds.

'Oi, there!' shouted his dad from below. 'What are you looking at? What's in that bag?'

'Nothing!' replied George. Passers-by were stopping to see what was going on.

'Is it a Spice Bag?'

Like seagulls, neighbours began to gather at the word *Spice Bag*.

'No! No, it's . . . fruit.'

Well, safe to say, that quickly got rid of the crowd.

'Well, hurry up and get that roof fixed before school!' roared his dad, slamming the front door behind him.

George did not know why, but in that instant, he cared little for the consequences and quickly swallowed down the golly-squash seeds. It may have been that his porridge was cold and unappetising and he was still hungry. But he was also tired and fed up of his parents. He had nothing to lose.

George braced himself. He waited for his face to bubble and bobble. And for his hands to turn different colours. And for his feet to burst from his runners. And a fatty, limp tail to sprout from his rear. But nothing happened. Not a thing.

'Morning, Georgie,' came the chirpy shout of his neighbour below.

'Hi, Jasper,' George replied, sounding a little deflated.

'You know, I prefer stargazing at night-time.'

'No. I was just . . . well, I'm supposed to be fixing the roof.'

'Ah, yes. Are you using porridge for cement? How creative!'

George climbed down from the roof and walked with Jasper to school. The two discussed the Playground Olympics enthusiastically on their way.

To George and his classmates, it was bigger than the real Olympics. By far. The winner of these games went down in playground folklore, and often on to super stardom.

'I'm definitely going to win the dance competition this year,' boasted Jasper. He produced a fold-up mop from his backpack. With a quick flick of the wrist, he flicked the mop out to its full extent. Using the mop to steady himself, he danced effortlessly from side to side, swivelling his hips and circling George with great co-ordination.

'Eh, we better get going if we want to make the start,' said George, changing the subject because in honesty he was very envious of Jasper's dance, which he felt had a very real chance of winning.

At their morning school assembly, Mr Benson stood at the front of the hall in his wedding dress (after all, Reader, a bet is a bet). You could tell that, unlike the students, this was his least favourite day of the year, and the vein on his forehead pulsated playfully.

'Right, everyone. Quiet down. Quieeeet . . . SHUT IT!' he roared and the assembly went silent.

'Now, we have quite a few events to get through this year, so let's not dilly-dally . . .' Mr Benson continued, massaging his forehead.

That's when George started to feel . . . *different*.

Not 'bad' different. Not at all, in fact.

George's tummy gurgled, and began to fizz and buzz. The sensation spread to his chest, then his arms and his hands and his fingertips. Soon his head was fizzing, and he was overcome with a profound and euphoric confidence. George felt capable of anything.

Chapter 11

Ms Smith, his favourite, and only, teacher got the games under way, igniting the Olympic flame with a lighter she had borrowed from one of her cats.

George was calm and confident, ambling from event to event. First, to the egg and spoon race where Ivy the Incredible, the reigning champion, strutted to the starting line. As Mr Benson's starter gun fired, and his vein jumped, so did Ivy to a quick start, breezing ahead effortlessly. She almost looked bored. But suddenly, like a greyhound from a trap, came our hero up the flank, right up through the finish line in first place. George had won by a Playground Olympic mile (around 10 metres) and posed for a photograph with a smug smile.

Next there was the dance off, which saw Jasper come a close second in a tear-jerking performance with his mop, to George's moon dance – a slick and smooth backwards slide – which the class watched through the astronomy club's special telescope as he danced on the actual moon.

After that came the spelling bee. The numbers quickly whittled down on some rather basic words posed by Ms Smith, the moderator, like 'my', 'cat', 'is', 'stuck', 'in', 'a', 'tree', 'outside', 'please', and 'help'. George was left as winner by default as his competitors followed Ms Smith to a tree outside. The school cheered manically for George, and Mr Benson was forced to play security guard as George-mania really took off.

The school cheered manically for George, and Mr Benson was forced to play security guard.

The last event was the pole-vaulting competition. It came down to George and Lanky Lawrence, or *Lanky Larry* as the school children fondly called him. Larry barely needed a pole to clear the horizontal bar, and the students applauded enthusiastically as the reigning champion helped Ms Smith get her cat from the tree.

Then up stepped the now-invincible George. He picked up his pole and, with the grace of a gazelle, vaulted effortlessly over the horizontal bar. *And* over the squishy mat on the other side. *And* over his adoring crowd. *AND* over the school gates! Up and up and up he soared. The cheers below were wild. As George flew from the school grounds like a cannon ball, he let out a joyous cry:

'WOOOOOOOOOOOOOOOOOOOOOAAAAAAA
AAAAAAAAAAAHOOOOOOOOOOOOOOOOO
OOOOOOO! I LOVE SPIIIIIIIIIIIIIIIIIIIIIIIIIIIIIIIIIIIIIIIIIIIIIIIICEEEEEEEEEEEEEEEEEEEEEES!'

CHAPTER
12

As he clambered from a bale of hay in the next field over, the new Playground Olympic Champion felt immensely chuffed. George could not wait to lap up his new-found stardom back at school. He was still buzzing from the golly-squash seeds. He even felt like he could do the games all over again.

This is only the beginning, he thought. With these spices, he could be the best at anything. Smarter than a teacher. Richer than a king. Stronger than a . . . Karl. The possibilities were endless.

On his way back to school, the rain began to fall heavily. George decided to shelter in a small wooded area nearby. He allowed his eyes to glaze as he relived his victory over and over. As the rain began to ease, he felt a *drip-drip-drip* on top of his head and his daydream was cut short.

George rubbed the top of his head. *That's not water.* He looked at the candle wax on his fingers and then directly above his head. For a moment he did not recognise the small, grubby boy up through the branches . . .

'Wax?' George peered up at the boy from the Council. 'What are you doing up there?'

'Creating a distraction,' said the boy, covered head to toe in green, red, and white wax.

Then Sweets caught George completely unaware, tackling him to the ground and sitting on top of him.

'What's going on?' cried George, trying to resist, but the golly-squash seeds had chosen an inconvenient moment to wear off.

Wax climbed down from the tree and stood over Sweets' shoulder. 'Well, Mr Playground Champion, what a superstar you are!' mocked Wax.

'Get off me!'

'You know, a champion like yourself must have a really good diet,' continued Wax, patting George's pockets. 'What do we have here?'

Wax pulled the brown-leather satchel from George's

pocket and poured the remaining golly-squash seeds into his hand.

'You know, where I come from, performance-enhancing spices aren't allowed,' said Wax furiously.

'They're mine! Give them back!'

'Barnaby wants to see you,' Sweets said calmly.

The three set off into the forest. Wax first, followed by George, being frog-marched by Sweets at the rear.

On arrival at the enormous Copper Beech tree, the atmosphere was different to his last visit. There was no noisy reception as before. No pots and pans. No screaming and howling. But George could feel a silent hostility pierce the air.

At the very top of the great tree, Sweets pushed George out into the breezy open air. The view was even more impressive during the day. Despite the rain clouds, he could make out the church steeple in the next town over and the green fields rolled into the distant horizon. George slowly approached the rest of the Elder Children.

'CHEATER!' Addy shouted, spotting him first.

'*How* did you beat Lanky Larry at the pole vault challenge?' Nerd asked racing up to him.

'It's just not possible!' Cry Baby wailed.

Sweets chewed his jellies slowly while Wax stood aside looking very pleased with himself indeed (you could probably already tell he had never quite taken to George).

The Elder Children's protests spilled over one another until—

WHACK!

Barnaby's walking stick slammed the impressive deck and the silence was instant. George had not noticed the 90-year-old-looking boy as the wrinkly leader's face had blended into the lined bark of the tree. Barnaby slowly sat back down on his cushion and gestured for George to step forward.

The wind whistled and the rain spat sideways. A few moments of calm passed before Barnaby spoke quietly, his eyes closed, his legs crossed.

'George, do you remember what we discussed at our last meeting?'

'Yes, of course, Barnaby.'

'I understand that you have now started working at Mr Spicebag's. What have you been doing there?'

George remembered Mr Spicebag's own warning about others wanting to exploit his gift.

Chapter 12

'Nothing. Just cleaning greasy floors really,' George muttered, avoiding Barnaby's gaze.

'What about Karl?' asked Barnaby, rising to his feet. 'Have you seen him?'

'No,' George muttered once more, squirming slightly. He could tell that Barnaby didn't believe him.

'George, let me remind you that it is my duty to protect *every* child in this town's welfare. Now, to that end, I'll ask you again. What have you been doing at Mr Spicebag's?'

The two locked eyes. Barnaby walked right up to George and whispered into his ear so that no one else could hear.

'I need to know, George. It is very important that I know what Mr Spicebag has been telling you.'

George said nothing. The silence hung in the air for what felt like an eternity.

'Very well,' Barnaby said in a clipped tone. 'For your lack of co-operation, I hereby disqualify you from the Playground Olympics.'

'That's not fair!'

'I decide what's fair! I am leader of these children! CHOSEN *BY* THESE CHILDREN!'

Mr Spicebag

There was little more to be said or done except for a good old-fashioned storm-out, and George's only regret was that there was no door to slam.

CHAPTER
13

George ran from the forest in a stormy rage. The weather was wild, which was fitting.

Who did that Barnaby think he was? Why would anyone listen to *them*? Council of the Elder Children? More like, Council of the Jealous Children. They couldn't stand that he, George, had won the Playground Olympics. He would show the lot of them. He just needed to get his hands on more of those spices . . .

Mr Spicebag's did not officially open for another hour, yet at that moment there was nobody else George wanted to talk to.

Soon he made out those familiar red fluorescent lights. Down the wet street he ran, not stopping until he reached Mr Spicebag's. Across the chipper floor and down the maroon patterned carpet, he swung open the basement door.

'Mr Spicebag!' George called, but there was no reply.

George was soaked from head to toe. His footsteps made odd squelching sounds as he walked down the steps.

'Mr Spicebag, helloooooOOOOO!'

Again, nothing.

George made himself at home. After all, he and Mr Spicebag were almost like partners. He ran all the way down the long tables, the odd page blown to the floor by his gusto. He swigged some leftover hot chocolate, which he quickly spat out into the fire. He ran over to Karl's cage and inspected the human-sized lizard.

'GIVE ME YOUR MONEY!' he mocked, banging the cage, rattling the enormous reptile.

He ambled alongside the old oak cupboards, trailing his fingertips on the chipped wooden doors. As he reached the second-to-last cupboard, the cupboard he recognised from the very first night (moved down to the basement to avoid any further meddling hands), he paused.

Now, Reader, although he felt angry like a wasp, he

thought twice before horning in. There was something about Mr Spicebag that made him double-check that the room was empty.

But then he considered Mr Spicebag further. *He* had proven to be the only person in George's life to appreciate him. And George had a hankering for some more spices. He wanted power and popularity, and he wanted to prove to everyone, especially that Council, that he *was* special. And so, he pulled open the rickety cupboard door.

There was quite a bit of dust in there and George felt a sneeze come on.

'AAAAAAAAA – Oh, wait false alar – AACHOOOO!'

Dust settled and he peered in. George could assure you that none of these spices resembled golly-squash seeds or glibbersnap dust or even feetrat seeds. Nope, not at all. They looked like any of the spices you might see in your spice rack at home. Like, rosemary and thyme, or oregano and paprika. Dill and turmeric, perhaps. Nothing special here.

George could not resist experimenting again and decided to give it a go using the three-step rule Mr Spicebag had taught him. *Smell* the spices. *Speak* to the spices. *Will* the spices.

George closed his eyes and took a few deep breaths, fully focused on what he desired, such was his rage. He imagined himself hoisted in the air by his classmates, holding the Playground Olympics trophy while the Council looked on in tears, begging on their knees for forgiveness.

Then, *veeery* gently, he took in delicate little sniffs.

Suddenly, a multitude of scents hit his nostrils thick and fast.

Sizzling bacon on a pan.

Burning rubber in the sun.

Fresh sea breeze on his face.

Just as he would recognise one, another would snatch his attention.

Steaming hot coffee.

Smoked pipe tobacco.

Warm peanut butter.

In no particular order, the smells came faster and faster, on and on, much more pungent now than they had been before.

George muttered too, just as Mr Spicebag had taught him, willing inspiration, willing the spices to achieve his desire . . .

Then he heard it.

A noise so barely audible, so remote that George thought it could have been a creak of the mind, and he nearly let it slide.

But then it came again, slightly sharper this time. From the very bottom shelf – a squeak, a chirp, or a pipe, or a peep.

Down on all fours, George peered in at a row of glass jars sheltered away in the paltry light. Curiously, these did not contain powders or dust, or ground leaves or beans, rather they were like sizeable chunks of roots wedged into small jars.

'Which one of you said that?'

Nothing.

'It's me, George. Come on, don't be shy,' he barely whispered. 'You can trust me . . . Who was it?'

Nothing but silence and darkness, and after some moments he was about to give up.

But then something in the corner of George's eye flickered fleetingly. He glanced over and in the far bottom right corner of the cupboard, a dirty jar behind all the others began to glow *ever* so slightly, just enough that it stood out.

George stretched in and took the jar out slowly. Carefully, he stood and inspected it. The jar was muddy. He could barely read the faint writing scrawled messily across the label. *Mortemtrip root.*

George twisted the lid off slowly to take a closer look. Roots bobbled on the surface reminding him of pickles in a jar, or a sneaky crocodile looking for its dinner.

Then from nowhere, a root flew out like a predator at its prey. The long, slimy root whipped around George's head so his screams were muffled. And out came another root and this time it slid around his arms. And another at his legs. George fought as best he could, but it happened far too fast. And then it went dark . . .

As if given a shot of adrenalin, George suddenly snapped his eyes open. He was being strangled mercilessly and could barely move his head. The long, thick roots gripped so tightly around his neck that he felt his head might explode. The roots continued to wrap themselves all around him like a great, death-dealing octopus. Tighter, and tighter, and tighter. Hope dwindled like water from a sponge, until George had no more fight to give.

CHAPTER
14

Then came a searing hot pain like a prod of lava being pressed against his chest. He had never felt such agony, but like a key it unlocked him. He could move again and he felt incredibly relieved.

And again, the burning seared him, and this time he managed to let out an ungodly roar.

'AAAAAAAAAAAAAAAHHHHHHHHHHH HHHHHHHHHHHHHHHHHHH!'

Again, burning scorched him, this time his leg. He let out another cry and jolted upright, his eyes wide with panic and pain.

The basement was almost unrecognisable. It now resembled a jungle, as vines, roots, and stems covered the floor and the walls and the ceiling. All the candlelight was gone, but the fire still smouldered. Just.

In front of him he could make out the unmistakable silhouette of Mr Spicebag branding and burning the roots with a red-hot poker (and George was sure he could hear the roots let out squeaks of pain as they contracted).

'Look at what you've done!'

'I–I–I–'

'This is not a game, George!' shouted Mr Spicebag, burning yet another root. 'You do not simply walk in here and dabble with these spices unattended!'

'I just thought—'

'You didn't think at all!' Mr Spicebag snapped, grabbing him firmly by the arm and holding the red-hot poker close to his face.

'This is not a cookery class, or a place to do little magic tricks,' said Mr Spicebag, the red of the poker reflected in his black eyes. 'This is an art; a science. Spices are living and complicated and dangerous. They must be harnessed. *Look* at this, George! It could have been so much worse had I not come back early.'

'But, I–I'm sorry . . . I just—'

'You *what?*' retorted Mr Spicebag, disgusted.

George opened his mouth but he was speechless.

'Just get out of my sight, George.'

Downtrodden and dejected, George stepped over the jungle-like steps.

'Oh, and George,' called up Mr Spicebag coldly. 'Not a word of this to anyone.'

The rain had eased, but it had turned dark and misty. It was getting late and most of his town were at home tucked into their Spice Bags.

George felt thoroughly sorry for himself. Playground Olympic Champion one minute, disqualification the next. However, worst of all was his banishment from Mr Spicebag's. Now he would never figure out the mystery surrounding the spices and all he could achieve with them.

He walked all the way to the outskirts of town where Karl had undergone his transformation. Eventually, his legs grew weary and the weather worsened. He turned back for home.

Neither the buses nor the trains were running at this hour, so he decided to take a shortcut through a nearby underpass. The tunnel crossed under a railway line and,

Chapter 14

while he could not see or hear anyone, he felt ill at ease. He paused and looked all around. The walkway was well lit and he could plainly see that no one was there.

And so, he started walking again, but this time he was *certain* that he heard an extra set of footsteps following him. He turned abruptly and could have sworn he saw a darting shadow. He exhaled the cold night air and inspected further, daring not to blink.

But not a thing.

George decided to scarper. He ran all the way down the windy passage and the second set of footsteps followed.

And as the end of the tunnel came in to view, he turned back to catch a glimpse of his pursuer. This, Reader, was a mistake because George was not looking as he turned the corner.

BAM!

CHAPTER
15

George saw stars.

Not stars you see in the sky at night-time, nor on the red carpet at the Oscars, but ones, as in this case, after a comprehensive whack.

'Watch where you're going!' came an angry voice.

His blurry vision came back into focus and he saw three, now two, now just the one little lady standing in front of him. She had hair like many mothers, short, curly, and ever so slightly greying. She was irritated and wore a yellow raincoat while nibbling at a Spice Bag.

'Sorry!' George blurted awkwardly. He glanced over his shoulder but nobody had followed.

'What do you think you're doing?' she snapped.

'Running into people at this hour of the night – you scared me half to death!'

The lady became teary.

'Are you OK?' George asked as she began to cry. 'I'm so sorry. I wasn't looking where I was going.'

The lady took a moment to calm herself.

'I shouldn't be so short with you.' She dabbed her eyes with a tissue. 'It's just, I'm looking for my son. Karl's his name. He's about your age.'

She produced a photograph of Karl. In the photo he stood unhappily in his school uniform while his mum smiled proudly alongside him. George hadn't thought that Karl might have a family who cared about him.

'He's been missing for days now,' she continued. 'I've been to the police but they're far too busy eating Spice Bags. I've asked his friends but they seem completely shaken by his disappearance. It's like he just . . . vanished off the face of the earth. And he's a good boy, really. Do you know, we enter a mother-and-son tap dancing competition together every year? We've won it the last two years in a row.'

George nearly smiled at this last bit. He took the

photograph to distract himself. He studied it, unsure of what to say.

'I hope he gets home safe,' he said, handing Karl's mum back the photograph.

She started to cry again.

'Oh, you better get home before *your* mum loses her head with worry,' she said, before stuffing the last piece of her Spice Bag into her mouth.

And with that, George walked away feeling ashamed. He had not for a second thought about Karl's family and how distraught they must be feeling – not knowing where their son or grandson had gotten to. George had been thinking only about himself and how the spices could improve his lot.

Then and there he made a resolution. To stop thinking about himself. To focus on turning Karl back. To do everything in his power to help Mr Spicebag. That is, of course, if Mr Spicebag ever forgave him.

To turn him back, Mr Spicebag needs to know how I turned Karl into a lizard. He thought hard. *What went into the Spice Bag that night?* What had he done that night that had turned Karl into a lizard?

George thought back to that night, that first night when

Chapter 15

he had gone to Mr Spicebag's. He had entered, he had broken a vase, he cleared up that vase, he cooked the food, he burnt himself, he found the cupboard, and the spices glowed vibrant colours of purple, orange, and green. But he had no clue, no recollection of what, or indeed what combination of, spices he had thrown in. He had simply gone on instinct. What was it about *that* Spice Bag that was so special? What was it about *that* Spice Bag that had turned Karl into a giant lizard?

He arrived at the end of his road, turning the corner onto the home straight. He fished his keys from his pocket. The lampposts lit his street sparsely and shadows draped all around.

It was then as he approached his gate that another shadow whisked past the corner of his eye, just like it had in the tunnel, and George stopped still. He peered into the darkness where the shadow had bolted.

'Hello?'

Nothing, but this time George crossed his quiet road to investigate.

Again, he thought he heard a noise and now he stopped dead still, barely breathing.

BANG!

A dustbin toppled and a stray cat dashed under a nearby parked car. George's heart nearly jumped from his mouth.

Terrified, he snatched his keys off the ground and walked quickly towards his gate.

'Georgie?'

George squinted up towards the neighbouring roof.

'Jasper!'

'I thought it was you I saw down there in the shadows talking to yourself.'

'What are you doing up there?'

'Stargazing. I know you prefer it in the morning with your porridge, but I find the stars easier to spot at this time of the day.'

Jasper stood atop a gable roof beside an impressive-looking telescope which was mounted on a tripod.

'Do you ever feel like you're being followed?'

'Sure, I do . . . Actually, come to think of it, no. Never. That sounds quite dodgy if you ask me, Georgie!'

Suddenly, a first-floor window from across the road opened. Mr Murphy, a large, tired-looking man stood at his window in his underpants. He had more hair on his back than George had on his entire head. He whisper-shouted across at them.

Chapter 15

'Will you two keep your voices down. You're going to wake the baby.'

'Hello, Mr Murphy,' Jasper shouted. 'Are you star-gazing tonight, as well?'

'Sssssssshhhhhhhh!' Mr Murphy plead-whispered. 'Quiet, you daft fool.'

'WHAT?!' Jasper roared. 'I CAN'T HEAR YOU!'

A baby's cries started from Mr Murphy's window.

'Oh, that's brilliant, just *brilliant*! Listen, if you two don't shut up, I'm going to get angry. And you *don't* want to see *me* angry.'

Mr Murphy shook an angry fist out his window. He must be cold, thought George (although the hair on his back looked quite warm).

'Oi! Bigfoot!'

Mrs Duffy had heard all the commotion, and had opened her window a few doors down from Mr Murphy's. She wore a dressing gown and hair curlers.

'Stay out of this, Dolores!' said Mr Murphy.

'Stay out of it? How can I stay out of it? All this racket at this hour!'

'It's these two muppets you should be annoyed with.

Roaring their heads off in the middle of the night, waking the baby!'

'Don't you blame them, Bigfoot!' Mrs Duffy shouted.

'*Don't* call me Bigfoot!'

This went on for quite a few minutes, Reader. More things were said. A grown man cried. The police were called.

George climbed onto the roof and sat down alongside Jasper who stood adjusting the telescope, peering through the eyepiece. The roof slates chilled his bottom.

'I need to find the ingredients that turned Karl into

122

a lizard, but I can't remember any of them. Not a single one.'

'Yes, that is quite a pickle,' Jasper said, peering through the telescope. 'Why don't you just tell her that you fancy her?'

'Jasper, are you paying any attention whatsoever?'

'Sure I am. You fancy Ms Smith.'

'What? No, Jasper, I don't!'

'I've seen how you look at her.'

'Jasper, we're getting off the point here. I'm talking about Karl. I've got to find out how I turned him into a lizard.'

'I remember a long, long time ago, when I was your age, Georgie, I was at a really very entertaining show.'

'What does this have to do with anything?' George rolled his eyes.

'There was this guy, a hypnotist, and he was absolutely brilliant!' Jasper continued. 'He had my grandad on stage. He got him doing all sorts of mad things, like clucking like a chicken, or eating like a pig from a trough, or singing the Albanian national anthem.'

'How do you know he was singing the Albanian national anthem?'

'How do you mean? The hypnotist told him to sing it, and so he did.'

'Yes, but was there anyone in the room who could confirm that your grandad was actually singing the Albanian national anthem and not just making it up?'

Jasper considered this point, but quickly brushed it away.

'The point is, Georgie, my grandad was able to access information that the hypnotist knew was stored deep inside his brain.'

George stared blankly at Jasper.

'Georgie, I am going to help you sing the Albanian national anthem.'

CHAPTER
16

'But what do you know about hypnosis, Jasper?'
'It's dead easy. All you need is an old pocket watch. Oh, and you have to be able to say, *"You're getting sleepy, veeery sleeeepy."*'

'It's just that simple,' said George sarcastically.

'Really, that simple.'

George rubbed his tired eyes. He didn't have much faith in Jasper, but then again, he had no better ideas.

'Sure. Why not.'

The two boys clambered into Jasper's attic bedroom through the roof window. Jasper carefully took apart his telescope and placed each piece into a box which he stored under his bed.

'Make yourself at home, Georgie. Can I get you anything?'

'No, thank you.'

George rubbed and blew into his hands to get some warmth.

'A bowl of hot vegetable soup perhaps?'

George's eyes lit up.

'Oh, actually, I'd *love* a bowl of hot vegetable soup.'

Jasper looked back uncomfortably.

'What is it?'

'I'm going to level with you, Georgie. I don't have any vegetable soup.'

'Then why did you ask if I wanted some?' asked George, slightly irritated.

'Honestly? Nobody has ever said yes. I mean, we're in an attic. For me to get you soup would involve me climbing down the ladder, going all the way down to the kitchen . . . most people wouldn't put me through the trouble of it all.'

'So, the hypnosis?'

'Yes, do have a seat, Georgie.'

George sat on the bed and Jasper pulled open a drawer of his writing desk. He picked out an old, golden pocket watch on a chain.

Jasper sat on the bed next to George.

Chapter 16

'OK, so – hypnosis. I'm going to level with you, Georgie. I've never done this before.'

'What?' He stood to leave.

'You see, I knew you would react like this, that's why I didn't tell you the truth!'

'I'm going home.'

'So how are you going to find the ingredients that turned Karl into a lizard?'

George did not know the answer to this question.

'Why not give it a chance?' urged Jasper. 'I've watched it online at least a half dozen times.'

George considered Jasper. He really was odd, but no other ideas came to mind. Not a single one.

'OK, let's give it a go.'

'Now, Georgie, I want you to take a few deep breaths. Inhale, exhale.'

'I know how to breathe.'

'OK, OK, Professor Breather. Deep breaths.'

George did as he was told.

'That's it, nice and calm. Listen to the sound of your breath.'

For a couple of minutes nothing was said. Jasper simply allowed George to be conscious of his breathing.

Eventually, Jasper dangled the golden pocket watch from its chain.

'Now, I want you to look at the watch, Georgie. That's it, look only at the watch.'

George did just that and, *ever* so slowly, Jasper began to sway the watch from side to side.

'Keep your eyes on the watch, only on the watch. Examine the hands – the hour hand, the minute hand, the second hand.'

For several minutes, Jasper allowed the watch to sway, letting its weight do the work.

While George was aware of his surroundings, he also felt relaxed, as if meditating. He focused only on the watch's hands, in particular the finer, longer 'second' hand, which he found most transfixing.

After some time passed, Jasper spoke again, but this time, a bit like a loud speaker at a train station, his voice echoed somewhat.

'Now, Georgie. You are getting sleepy, *veeery* sleepy. Your eyes are getting heavy, *veeery* heavy.'

And as Jasper spoke these words, George did indeed feel his eyes weigh down, and they drooped a little more until they were fully closed. He was in a tranquil, restful state.

Chapter 16

'I want you to think back, Georgie. Think back to that night when Karl was turned into a lizard. Where were you coming from before Mr Spicebag's?'

'School,' answered George, sleepily, eyes closed.

'And what happened at school?'

'Ms Smith gave me turnip seeds.'

'So kind. Now I see why you fancy her.'

'I don't fancy her.'

'Let's move on. What happened then?'

'Karl.'

'What about Karl?'

'He tried to eat my turnip seeds.'

'And how did that make you feel?'

'Mad. Really mad. Scared too.'

'Why scared?'

'Karl always scares me. He's huge. Says he'll kill me.'

'OK . . . OK, now Georgie. What happened after Karl?'

'I had to go to Mr Spicebag's.'

'Right. Yes, now I want you to picture Mr Spicebag's, and I want you to imagine you are holding the finished Spice Bag – the one Karl ate. What does it look like?'

'Soggy.'

'What else?'

'Nothing, just soggy.'

'Ok. Take a step back then . . . Where exactly did you put the spices onto the food?'

'At the cupboard.'

'Where?'

'The cupboard in the back hallway, at the top of the basement stairs.'

'Good. And what was the last ingredient that went on to the food?'

Then George was there, right outside the basement door. He was brought right back to that night, to the making of the Spice Bag that transformed Karl. It was like he was watching a home video of himself, of that glorious moment when he had been at one with the spices, when raw instinct prevailed.

There was, however, something odd about this replay of events.

George was watching in rewind. So, it felt like he was watching a film that started at the end with the finished Spice Bag and went backwards, almost in slow motion. The colours were just as clear and impressive as they had been, except strangely it looked as though all the spices were going *from* the Spice Bag back into their jars, rather than the other way round. Absolutely bizarre, but it was as clear as day. Including the labels on the jars.

'Smidge root,' George blurted, having said nothing for at least a minute.

'Smidge root?' asked a puzzled Jasper, scrawling the words down on a page.

George continued to watch himself in this home video.

The scents came flying back too. One like fruit, another like wet clothes. One like freshly cut grass, then a smell of burnt toast. The one that reminded him of Christmas and one that gave off a powerful smell of snot (a smell which George now knew existed). Again, one smelled like his vegetable patch while another reminded him of a Sunday years before when he was much smaller and his family argued a lot while playing Monopoly, but they were happy.

'Wincer-snoodle spice.'

Jasper took note, watching on in amazement.

'Ground chizzlestone.'

'Brilliant, Georgie, keep going!'

'Shnipton seeds.'

And this went on for a number of minutes, an hour maybe, it is hard to say. George would take breaks, as if snoozing, and then blurt out the name of a spice.

'Larsnidge extract.'

Jasper kept encouraging him. It was working – he had already written down two dozen spices.

'Rashpine spice.'

'Windflop shake.'

'Golly-squash seeds.'

'Finelpop powder.'

Then silence.

George slouched, limp, sapped of all energy.

'Georgie?'

Jasper patted George's face lightly.

'Georgie? Is that it?'

Jasper shook George's elbow slightly, and George made a disagreeable sound, as if cranky at being woken from a slumber (which I suppose, in a way, he was).

'Georgie. Are you finished? Are there any other spices that go in?'

'No,' George replied, almost unconscious.

'No? No, you're not finished? Or no more spices went into the Spice Bag?'

Chapter 16

George began to snore. Jasper was about to give up, folding the piece of paper with the recipe.

'Blood!'

'Blood? Georgie, what are you talking about?'

'Blood from the vase.'

'Blood from the vase? What does that mean, Georgie?'

'The vase at Mr Spicebag's, on the counter . . . near the front door.'

Jasper looked baffled, but allowed George to continue.

'I cut my hand on the broken vase.'

Jasper looked down at George's limp hands. He turned them over and, sure enough, on his right palm there was a long scratch. A thin, bloody scab.

'Georgie,' Jasper muttered quietly. 'You've done it. You can open your eyes.'

He snapped his fingers to wake George.

SNAP!

CHAPTER
17

'Must have nodded off,' said George, rubbing his eyes. 'Right, shall we give this hypnosis thing a go?'

He looked at Jasper, who was unusually speechless.

'What is it?'

'Georgie, are you telling me you don't remember any of the last hour?'

'I was asleep for an hour?!'

Jasper handed the list to George in shock.

'What's this?'

'I . . . I think we've done it.'

'Done what?'

'You went into a weird, sleepy trance and . . . Georgie,' he grabbed George by the shoulders, 'I really think you listed the recipe that turned Karl into a lizard.'

George looked at Jasper, then at the list in Jasper's hand. They stood in total amazement.

'We did it,' said George to himself, taking the list. 'We did it!'

The two boys didn't know what to do with themselves. So, of course, they jumped to their feet and screamed like lunatics.

'YEEEEES!' cried George, and then over to the window which he pulled open, letting out another roar into the cool night air.

'WOOOOOOOOOHOOOOOOOOOOOOOO!'

Then Jasper joined him at the window and they both let out yells and whistles of joy.

'Oi!'

Mr Murphy seethed at his bedroom window as a baby cried in the background. 'What is WRONG with you two!'

'Oi, Bigfoot!' came Mrs Duffy's voice.

'Stay out of this, Dolores!'

The two boys got a hold of themselves and slammed the window shut. George stared at the list.

'I don't know what to say, Jasper.'

He read through the list of ingredients.

'Blood?'

'It was the last thing you said.'

Jasper turned George's hand, showing him the scratch on his palm.

'The vase . . . I broke the vase,' muttered George. 'I must have nicked my hand when I was clearing it up!'

'You mean . . . *blood* is an ingredient?' asked Jasper, slightly sickened.

'I don't know,' said George. 'But I'm going to find out.'

George walked quickly to the window.

'Wait, where are you going?'

'To Mr Spicebag's, of course! This can't wait!'

'It's the middle of the night, Georgie. I know you like doing things slightly differently, what with your daytime stargazing and so on, but can't it wait until morning?'

'It really can't. Mr Spicebag said if he has this recipe, he'll be able to turn Karl back.'

'But, Georgie, you said you were being followed!'

'It's a risk I need to take. Mr Spicebag needs to know now.'

'Wait!'

George looked back at Jasper.

Chapter 17

'I'll come with you. Ms Smith would never forgive me if I let anything happen to you.'

George smiled at his friend who, he decided, deserved a lot more credit than he sometimes gave him.

* * *

In no time at all, the two boys were a stone's throw from the chipper. It was quiet, except for the wind that was getting wilder by the minute, and some local drunks in the distance also, by the sound of it, getting wilder by the minute. The street glistened under the bright red writing that read 'Mr Spicebag's'. This light, by contrast, made the shadows appear even darker.

As the boys approached the chipper door, there came a sharp whistle from the darkness. There stood a tall, shady figure in the shadows and, although it was too dark to see, George knew. Do not ask him how or why, but he knew that this had been his pursuer in the tunnel before he collided with Karl's mum, *and* on his street before he had met Jasper earlier that night.

'What do you want?' called George, squirming nervously.

No reply.

'You were following me through the tunnel too. *And* down my road! I can see you, you know, I'm not stupid!'

For a moment, it seemed like the figure had chosen to ignore them, and George had to admit that he was quite relieved by this, his bravery having dwindled by the second.

But then the towering stranger began to walk slowly from the shadows. This person was far too wide to be Mr Spicebag (whose outline resembled a nearby lamp-post).

As if in a horror film, the man clomped somewhat unnaturally towards them. George's belly lurched in fear and he darted for the chipper door. But Jasper stood his ground.

'Jasper!'

'My grandad has a black belt in karate and taught me a few moves. Get inside, Georgie! I'll take care of this.'

But George would not have it. His friend had proven loyal to him and now it was his turn. He ran up behind Jasper and pulled him in through the chipper door with every ounce of strength he could muster.

'But, Georgie.'

'Don't argue, just follow me. Now, Jasper!'

Through the chipper, down the hallway, George swung open the basement door.

'In! Quickly!'

Jasper began to protest but George ushered his friend into the basement, locking the door.

CLICK!

George looked down at Mr Spicebag who stared right back up at them in surprise. The fire was roaring. The table and the chairs, and the bookshelves and the spice cupboards, were all back where they should be.

'What are you doing here?' asked Mr Spicebag in shock.

'I've got to tell you something!' called George, quickly descending the long set of stone steps.

'I told you not to tell ANYONE!'

George stopped abruptly, taken aback by this sudden anger. He had not seen Mr Spicebag like this before. Even when George had turned the basement into a jungle, Mr Spicebag had just seemed really disappointed.

'What did I tell you – I *told* you not to tell a SOUL!' yelled Mr Spicebag.

Suddenly those long, pin-needle-like legs made their way up the stairs furiously, five steps at a time.

'Do you know what we're doing here?' yelled Mr Spicebag. 'Do you have any idea?'

Mr Spicebag fast approached, those long arms swaying from side to side. George felt fear rise from his stomach.

But then he lunged for Jasper, reefing the boy off his feet, throwing him down several steps so that he landed painfully at the bottom.

Jasper began to weep uncontrollably. The closer Mr Spicebag got down to him, the louder the poor boy cried.

'Leave him alone, it's my fault, not his!' shouted George, but he was ignored.

Jasper's screams grew louder, his cries strangely high pitched. And then the cries downgraded to sobs, his face glistening with tears. Then . . . laughter? George wondered what an earth he was thinking.

Mr Spicebag grabbed Jasper by the collar with both hands. He pulled back a hand to strike him hard . . .

'HE *REMEMBERED*!' Jasper blurted from his tear-soaked face. His eyes were wide and he beamed deliriously from ear to ear.

'What are you talking about *now*, you fool?'

'We have the recipe, Grandad!'

CHAPTER
18

Grandad? Jasper, what are you talking about?' George asked, but he already knew the answer.

Jasper lay on his back, laughing hysterically. George had never heard him laugh like this before. It was shrill and unsettling. His face also shifted subtly so that it took on a slightly manic appearance.

'Silence!'

Jasper immediately obeyed, although he continued to smirk.

'Sit, *Georgie*,' directed Mr Spicebag, pointing to a chair near the roaring fire.

'What's going on, Jasper?' George asked nervously, sitting as told.

'*What's going on, Jasper?*' mimicked Jasper.

Mr Spicebag began to applaud, as if to get attention.

'Well done, George.' He walked over and extended his twig-like fingers. 'The recipe. *Please.*'

'Jasper, we're friends!' cried George, Mr Spicebag snatching the page from his hand. 'What's going on?'

'*Friend* is a bit of a strong word, isn't it?' considered Jasper. 'A neighbour. A colleague. An associate, perhaps. Even a comrade . . . Actually, yes, come to think of it, I suppose I did rather stab you in the back, didn't I? Oh well.'

'Mr Spicebag is your grandad?'

'Ladies and gentleman, he finally gets it!' mocked Jasper in a rather impressive American accent, shouting up to the ceiling as if presenting a television show, his voice echoing, 'Please, let's give him a round of applause!'

'Keep it down!' barked Mr Spicebag, reading an old book with his monocle. Jasper obeyed but he continued to smirk menacingly at George.

So many questions simmered on the surface of George's tongue.

'But why the secrecy? Why does it matter who knows he's your grandad?'

Jasper thought a moment before answering.

Chapter 18

'The less information the public has the better. Simple as that, Georgie. I am grandad's eyes and ears in this town.'

'Wait a second,' George said, his mind racing. 'When you crashed your granda— Mr Spicebag's car . . . were you following me?'

'Well, we couldn't just let you get away once you'd discovered our spices.'

George struggled to take this all in.

'You see, Georgie,' continued Jasper, beaming broadly. 'Me and grandad have been working on our little project for a long time. And now that we have the recipe . . . well, we can finally open our zoo.'

George's thoughts were bouncing around his brain like a frenzied tennis ball.

'Hang on. When I was here that first night, that night that I made the Spice Bag that transformed Karl, *you* were here. *You* were the other voice!'

Jasper grinned widely like a Cheshire cat.

'Jasper,' Mr Spicebag shouted from across the room. 'Over here. Now!'

Jasper gave George one last fleeting smile. It was only then that George realised the resemblance between Jasper and Mr Spicebag. Although his hair was auburn rather than peppery, his eyes too were dark and beady, his frame tall, and George felt quite surprised, foolish even, that he had not seen the likeness before.

Jasper took instructions and obediently began to assemble various jars from the cupboards.

'Now, George,' smiled Mr Spicebag. 'I must ask you, please, to put your hands behind the chair.'

Mr Spicebag quickly began to tie George's arms and legs to the chair.

'What's going on? I thought you said you could turn Karl back if we found the recipe!'

'I'm afraid,' he said, standing straight, 'that was a white lie.'

'White lie. What are you talking about?!' shouted a now immobile George.

'For a start, I suggest that you *watch your tone*,' Mr Spicebag said in a threatening voice.

George went silent.

'It's people like you,' continued Mr Spicebag, 'horrible, meddlesome people like you that started all this . . .'

'Hey!' blurted George.

'Hey *WHAT?*' snapped Mr Spicebag through gritted teeth.

Chapter 18

'These spices,' he continued, gesturing towards the cupboards, 'are not simply spices that you can buy in a supermarket. They are the culmination of many, many years . . . nay, many, many *generations* of research and cultivation. These spices are the fruit of a toil that you will never understand.

'You see, our family is a very, *very* ancient family indeed. My great, great, great, great, great, great, great – well, you get the idea – my ancestors had a plan. A plan which I have made my life's mission to fulfil.'

Mr Spicebag ambled around, enjoying the sound of his own voice.

'Have you ever looked around at what this world has become, George? Have you seen what all these snappy, snarly, yappy people have done to this planet? It's a mess. My ancestors knew it then and it's ever truer now. Humankind is poison. Anything humans touch with their greedy paws withers and dies eventually . . . well, I intend to change all that. Thanks to you.'

'Thanks to me?'

'What is the solution to this destructive greed?' asked Mr Spicebag rhetorically. 'Well, George, here's a clue – maybe if humans are going to *act* like animals, then they should be *treated* like animals. And if they are to be *treated* like animals . . . well, there's only one way to properly make that happen.

'Have you ever imagined a world *without* humans, made up entirely of animals?' he deliberated. 'What would that be like? Chaotic for a time, perhaps, but no more greed-driven humans grasping and guzzling everything they touch, ruining more than their fair share. Just animals going about their business . . . Well, I think you understand what I'm getting at.'

'No, I don't understand! What are you saying?'

'Well, it's very simple,' Mr Spicebag said. 'Turn most humans into animals, leaving a select few – me, and those whom *I* deem worthy – to run the show. I shall start over; it will be a new beginning where *I* top the food chain. As I already rule this town with my food, I dare say that this should be quite the straightforward task indeed. And if anyone has any complaints, they can answer to *me*.'

'But that's impossible!'

'Correction, George. We *thought* it was impossible. For generations my family tried. My own grandfather managed to perfect the useful, and indeed *addictive* component – golly-squash seeds, in fact. How do you think I managed to get *you* on side? And what better place to experiment than by opening a place where greed congregates: a chipper! But I was missing the vital combination of ingredients. Until now . . .'

He paused for dramatic effect.

'Blood. So clear to me now, but that's just the nature of hindsight I suppose, isn't it? I cannot simply *will* the spices to work, my desire *alone* is not sufficient. My intention must be in the form of a physical manifestation. An actual part of me. It is so *obvious* now.

'It will take some getting used to, of course. We'll need to see who turns into what. Some animals will prove redundant, like rats, or turtles, or tapeworms – we'll exterminate those immediately. But others, like horses and pigs and cattle, for example, will have their use for labour and meat and milkshakes, and the like. At least then, George, *then* humankind, naaaaay, *animalkind* shall be of some use to me.'

'What? But why would you do this?'

'Yes, I know what you might be thinking – why go to the trouble of it all? Why not simply poison everyone? Well, that had crossed my mind, George. But that would be preposterous and I'm no monster. No, they will each have their chance. As long as they are useful to me as animals, they will be spared. Soon, every man, woman, and child in the country will be turned to beast. And after that there will be no stopping us.'

'Yeah, no stopping us!' rallied Jasper, appearing along-side Mr Spicebag.

'You're completely, barking mad. Both of you. You won't be able to do this – I won't help you anymore!'

'Ha! I don't need you,' Mr Spicebag said. 'There's nothing special about *you*. Any fool could do what you did. You won the lottery.'

The fire crackled, breaking the silence.

'The ingredients are ready, Grandad.'

Mr Spicebag considered George for one more brief moment before walking away.

'Oh, Georgie, cheer up,' Jasper said. 'It's not *all* bad. No more school or homework, or nasty parents telling you what to do . . . I hope you turn into a useful animal though, Georgie, I really do.'

'You're *crazy!*'

'Oh, no, no. No, Georgie,' said Jasper with a smile. 'No, I'm not crazy. No, you're just upset. Hey, maybe you'll turn into a dog. Man's best friend, how does that sound? Then we'll see who's barking mad.'

'Jasper!' snapped Mr Spicebag.

George sat helplessly as the two traitors arranged the ingredients under candlelight. Mr Spicebag dropped the first ingredient into the mortar and began to grind the spices slowly, whispering secretly. Jasper was also muttering something while he worked alongside his grandad.

'Wincer-snoodle spice,' instructed Mr Spicebag, and Jasper added a teaspoon carefully.

Mr Spicebag continued to grind the spices. For several minutes, they muttered together, almost like they were anointing something – it seemed almost religious. Every so often Mr Spicebag would instruct Jasper to pass him an ingredient, or to place in a dash or a pinch or a spoonful of a spice, and the boy would oblige.

George waited in angst. His tied fists clenched, his arms tense, he could feel something was about to happen.

True to his gut, George could see faint light and movement in the mortar from across the room. The dim light emanated brighter, and he could hear the sound of grains swirling.

'Larsnidge extract,' Mr Spicebag said, and Jasper added a fair helping into the mix, and this really made a difference.

The twister of spices rose higher from the bowl. With each ingredient it became more pronounced in shape, fuller in colour. Black and grey and white, it spun faster and faster. And the faster it spun, the brighter it became. So much so that Mr Spicebag's methodical spice-grinding wrist and arm was illuminated, and it became windy, *very* windy.

'Windflop shake and finelpop powder. Quickly, Jasper!' ordered Mr Spicebag.

The twister grew louder and louder, higher and higher up towards the ceiling.

'Now, Jasper! The knife. Take the knife and draw blood.'

Jasper took the knife and turned towards George.

'Not him, you fool!'

And now the noise of the twister was deafening. It began to destroy everything in its path. The long table was flung backwards against the wall, narrowly missing George's head. The cupboard doors slammed open and hundreds of spice jars smashed to the floor, but neither Mr Spicebag nor Jasper cared.

Chapter 18

Jasper slashed his grandad's thumb, and blood dripped from the twig-like hand into the twister. Mr Spicebag's blood was like petrol to a fire. The room was lit up by swirling red, orange, and yellow flames which grew so high that they looked like they would set the wooden chandelier on the ceiling alight and the entire building with it.

The flames began to singe and scorch. George could feel his face burn unbearably. And just when it appeared as if Mr Spicebag could not possibly continue to grind the spice mix any further (because it really did seem like he was about to disappear into the twister at any moment), there was an almighty *FLASH!*

For several moments, George thought he was a goner as there was nothing at all but silence and bright, white light.

But then came a ringing in his ear. The white turned to a blur, and he could hear an odd, high-pitched laugh. The smell of burning grease was overwhelming and white smoke filled the room.

'We have it,' Mr Spicebag cried. 'I *know* we have it. I've finally done it!'

Jasper's unnerving laughter rang up through the room. As George regained full vision, the room appeared sideways. In actual fact, it was he who lay awkwardly on his side, still tied to his chair.

'We need to try this out on someone.'

'What about him?' Jasper suggested and laughed.

The two stared across the room at George, who lay helplessly. Mr Spicebag walked over and stared at George pensively.

'Not him. We may need him yet. But . . . I think our best customers might be more than happy to assist.'

'Best customers, Grandad?'

'Why George's parents, of course.'

'NO!' George shouted. 'Please, leave them out of this!'

George surprised himself at how protective he was of his parents.

'Please, Mr Spicebag. You don't want to use them. If you feed it to them, then the secret will be out and you don't want that yet!'

'You know what, George. That's not a bad point . . .' considered Mr Spicebag. 'But quite frankly, I don't care. Come on, Jasper, to George's house.'

Chapter 18

'No. Please. Come back,' George screamed. 'Don't *touch* my family!'

But his protests were in vain as the two left on their merry way, locking the door behind them.

George tried with all his might to break free from the chair but it was hopeless.

'Heeeeeelp!'

But nobody came.

'HEEEEEEEEEELP!'

It was then, as all looked lost, that the pitter-patter of tiny feet grew louder.

'Gggeorge?'

CHAPTER
19

'Gggeorge, why are you, 'ow you say, *crying*?' asked the rodent.

'Maurice, you've got to help me!'

'*Oui*, yes, of course. But first, do you 'av any food? Ze walnuts, perhaps?'

'No, I've nothing. Look, I don't have time to explain, but Mr Spicebag and Jasper, they're evil. They plan on turning everyone into animals!'

'Oh, I knew zat zey were up to somezing . . . But, ugh, more importantly, rallay, you 'av nuzing to eat, non? Zum eggs, maybe? An omelette?'

'What? Look at me. I'm tied to a chair, why would I have an omelette to give you?'

'Well, maybe zum, 'ow you say, Tic Tacs?'

George stared at the mouse. Maurice stared at George.

'I think I have some Polo mints in my pocket.'

Maurice dived into George's back pocket and returned with a Polo mint, which looked more like a life ring in his paws. The mouse munched it down quickly.

'Ah, zat ees much bettuur. Merci, zank you,' Maurice said with the freshest breath a mouse has ever 'ad.

'Maurice, please you've got to get me out of here.'

'Ba, *oui*, of curse, ma friend.'

The mouse grinned, showing two rather sharp-looking front teeth, and without further hesitation darted for George's ankles. In a few short minutes, George's feet and legs were freed. Next, Maurice ran around to George's hands and arms, chomping as fast as he could. Just as freedom seemed a few short bites away, a sound came from the door high above.

'Maurice, hurry,' George whispered. 'They're coming back.'

The mouse nipped and bit with all his might, but it was too late. The door pushed open and George recognised the figure instantly. The tall, broad man who he had seen skulking in the shadows outside earlier peered down at him. George's gut lurched.

George rose to his feet, but his hands remained tied to the chair behind his back. He backed away until the chair hit the wall behind him – he had nowhere left to go.

'Do not wurry, Gggeorge! I shall defend you!'

The mouse bounded up the steps and out of sight, for it was dark and he was small. The mysterious man took each step carefully as there was no light to show him the way. It was then that the figure stopped in his stride. Suddenly he began to wriggle and to shake all over like he was performing some odd dance.

'MOUSE!' the man screamed, although his voice did not match his imposing figure one little bit.

Then, there's no easy way to describe this, Reader. He began to come apart. It was one of the oddest scenes George had ever witnessed. First the hat fell, then his entire body seemed to topple in every direction, tumbling in a heap down the stairs. It was a noisy commotion – too noisy for one man.

'Somebody get a light!' came a recognisable voice.

A candle lit up and a short, grubby boy came into view. His face glowed above the candle, and a wave of relief overcame George.

'Wax!'

The small Elder boy was joined by the other members of the Council. First Sweets came forward, then Addy, followed by Nerd and Cry Baby. Heidi was harder to spot as usual but stepped from the darkness. Last, and most certainly not least, the elderest Elder of the lot, Barnaby, hobbled forward with a walking stick. George was ecstatic and would have embraced them all had his arms not been attached to the chair.

'Barnaby, I'm so sorry,' George said. 'I was such a fool.'

Barnaby held up his hand.

'Now is not the time, George. Are you OK?'

'Mr Spicebag and Jasper. They're evil! Mr Spicebag is Jasper's grandad. They're going to turn the whole town into animals!'

Cry Baby began to cry. The other Elders gasped – all but Barnaby, who took it in his stride.

'Wait . . . How did you know I was here?'

'We've been following you,' Wax said. 'Ever since you miraculously won the Playground Olympics, we knew something wasn't right, you cheater.'

'George,' Barnaby said, 'I'm afraid that I have had my doubts about Mr Spicebag for some time. His effect on this town is plain to see, but I must admit that I did *not* think it would be this bad. We had to follow you – it was a necessary evil.'

'Ah-he-he-heeem,' Maurice cleared his throat. 'Gggeorge, aren't you, uh, going to introduce me?'

'Oh, sorry. Everyone, this is Maurice, he can talk.'

The group looked on, stunned. Cry Baby whimpered.

''Av you, ugh, anyzing to eat, ma friends?'

Sweets pulled out a brown paper bag and handed the mouse a jelly fried egg.

'Ah, an egg! Not an omelette, but vurry close,' Maurice said as he chewed the delicious treat.

'Just one thing,' asked George. 'How did you manage to follow me? What I mean is, you could hardly walk straight piled on top of one another . . . how were you able to follow me down the tunnel when I met Karl's mum? Or on my street?'

They all stared at Heidi.

'Like I said before, George,' Barnaby said. 'Heidi is the best at hide-and-go-seek. Without her, we would all be lost.'

Even though the room was barely lit, George could see Heidi blush.

Chapter 19

'Now, everyone,' Barnaby said. 'We need to act fast. Where were Mr Spicebag and Jasper going?'

'To my house. They're going to test the new spice mix out on my parents,' George said as Wax burnt the rope away from his wrists.

'And what about this zoo?'

George grabbed a flyer from the long table and handed it to Barnaby.

'It says that there's a big party at the zoo to celebrate Mr Spicebag's birthday and there'll be free Spice Bags for all,' George replied. 'This is bound to attract the whole town.'

'You're right,' considered Barnaby. 'Right, Heidi, go to the zoo and find out what's going on, then meet us at George's house as fast as you can.'

'Sure thing,' Heidi said and off she shot.

'The rest of you, to George's house.'

'What about him?' George asked, pointing at Karl in the brass cage.

'Addy, Cry Baby, guide Karl,' ordered Barnaby. 'We can't have him running off – we need to get him home.'

'But he's looking at me all funny,' said Cry Baby.

'Fine. Addy, can you take him?'

'You betcha, Barnaby!'

Addy opened the cage door, darted around Karl, and put him on all fours. She tied a rope comfortably around him and rode him effortlessly, like an experienced cowgirl.

'OK, everyone, have we got everything?' asked Barnaby.

'Wait!' George ran over to the sideways storage cupboards and after a moment appeared with a small bag of golly-squash seeds. 'Mr Spicebag said these were addictive. Might come in useful. Not sure how . . . call it instinct.'

'Excellent, George. Right, let's go!'

The group looked like a marching band without the instruments as it made its way through the small town. A 90-year-old-looking boy with a walking stick at the front, a small frizzy headed girl on a giant lizard at the back, and a crew of all shapes and sizes in between (not forgetting Maurice, happily chewing the jelly fried egg on George's shoulder). Although they did not know what to expect at his house, George felt the safest he had felt in a long time. Almost as if he was part of a family again.

Chapter 19

They travelled in silence, focused on their task ahead. As he turned his front door key, George turned back and gave them a look as if to say, 'Brace yourselves.' Ever so slowly he opened the door, willing it not to creak. But there was no need to be quiet as the house was in a state of *absolute pandemonium.*

It was obvious that George's dad had been holding an early-morning court as the house was full of hardened criminals. But they were acting anything *but* hardened as they ran around, screaming like little babies (no offence if you happen to be a little baby, Reader – it's really just a turn of phrase).

The odd-looking group made their way into the hallway. From the sitting room they could hear the sound of, first, crying, and, second, snarling. George pushed open the door to find two huge grizzly bears growling in the face of a bunch of criminals who cowered behind Fran, the apple-pinching gran.

Fran kept the bears at bay with her Zimmer frame outstretched in front of her like a lion-tamer's chair.

'STAY BACK, YOU GREAT BRUTES!'

Men twice Fran's size and half her age bawled crying, using the old-age pensioner as a human shield.

'Fran!'

'Ah, George!' Fran said with a smile, as if defending herself from two grizzly bears was perfectly normal. 'How have you been, dear?'

George ignored the question as the bears roared even louder into the little old lady's face.

It was then George realised that one of the bears wore his dad's judge's wig, while the other wore his mum's open-toed sandals.

The awful realisation hit him hard.

'DAD! MUM!' George yelled, and the two bears looked down at their son.

For a moment it seemed as though they recognised him. But then animal instinct took over, and they both let out an almighty *RROOOOOAAAAAARRRR!*

CHAPTER
20

His dad aimed a powerful paw at George's head, but took out a defenceless lamp on the side table instead.

SMASH!

Now his mum bounded at George from across the room on all fours. He darted from the doorway – just in time too as the mother bear collided hard with the wall where he had just stood.

CRASH!

'OOOOOOOOOOHHHHHHH!' came the prisoners' groans, like the audience at a wrestling match.

His mum left a huge bear-shaped hollow in the wall. The impact caused the room to rumble and tiny pieces of the ceiling to crumble.

George turned to face the gang, who had remained in the hallway.

'Stay back!' he warned them. 'Mum, Dad, over here.'

The two bears stepped up their pursuit and it really did look as though they were going to eat their son after all. Maybe his dad would finally follow through on his threats. They bounded towards the sitting-room door and became momentarily wedged together in the door frame. That is, until his dad managed to push through and chase George down to the kitchen, knocking over the hall table with his enormous hairy bottom.

George ran through the kitchen towards the back door. In his haste he had forgotten how slippery the floor had become from all the discarded greasy paper bags. He slid into the fridge. Now it was his turn to make a rather loud **CRUNCH!**

The bears bundled into the kitchen and slid across the floor. They reminded him of two synchronised figure skaters on ice, except figure skaters (usually) wore ice skates and (normally) did not want to eat 10-year-old boys.

His parents had been momentarily stalled in their pursuit, but they soon got their bear-ings (get it, Reader?), standing tentatively on their paws on the slippery surface. His mum, being the (ever so slightly) nimbler of the two, leapt first, trapping her son with a paw the size of a tennis racket. Again, she roared and looked as though she might just scoff him down in one go for her breakfast.

CRACK!

The mother bear whimpered away from her son. His dad too had been startled by the noise and momentarily backed off. George opened his eyes to see Lucy standing over him with the remainder of yet another innocent lamp.

'Lucy!' It was unusual to see Lucy hold anything but her mobile phone.

'George! Are you OK?!' It was also unusual to hear Lucy speak; she only texted and blew impressive bubbles.

'Lucy, quick, into the garden!'

They ran into the garden but quickly became separated. Lucy, being much taller, managed to pull herself onto a low-hanging branch to safety. George kept running, and the bears followed, gaining on their mouth-watering son.

Past his small greenhouse he ran, all the way to the back of the garden. Now George really was about to hit a dead end as the back garden wall loomed ahead. His parents were gaining on him fast. Bears can run remarkably quickly, Reader, especially when chasing a delicious 10-year-old child.

As George reached his vegetable patch, he looked back over his shoulder. Again, this was a mistake, and he tripped face-first into the soil. He had nowhere to run. Nowhere to hide. No big sister to save him.

Frantically, he pulled himself backwards along the soil as his two grizzly bearants bounded towards him. In desperation, he began to pull up vegetables beneath him as he squirmed backwards, flinging them at the beasts.

Chapter 20

It all looked quite helpless as the two gigantic beasts advanced for a well-earned snack. It was then by chance that George threw a carrot down his dad's throat like a hole-in-one, while his mum mistook a parsnip for a finger and chomped a bite.

Curiously, they paused in their pursuit.

All of a sudden, the bears became much less interested in George. They lay peacefully in the flower bed and began to gnaw the uprooted vegetables. George watched on in amazement, afraid to move even a muscle.

The bears munched happily, his dad a fan of carrots, while his mum preferred parsnips. Lucy looked on amazed from the low-hanging branch while George simply shrugged his shoulders back at her.

Then George realised that the vegetables had proved to be an antidote of sorts. Yes, his parents were still bears, but they were much less eager to eat their only son.

But just as George was beginning to let his guard down, the bears suddenly became ill at ease, rising to their feet. They were irritable, so George quickly crawled behind a nearby bush. He sat with his back to the shrub, not daring to peer back over in case he was seen.

The bears stood on their hind legs, facing each other as if ready to fight. They circled round and round, snarling at one another. Suddenly, they began to diminish in size. They got smaller and smaller, their fur gave way to hair, and finally their features morphed.

FLASH!

George looked up and was absolutely horrified at the sight before him. For his parents were not bears anymore, but humans. Naked humans. George's parents now faced each other in the same bear-clawed stance except now they were just Mum and Dad, and entirely in the nip. They looked like they were coming out of a very strong spell (or a particularly heavy Spice Bag binge). Their eyes focused and it dawned on them that they were standing naked in the back garden with neighbours peering in.

His mum let out a shriek and his dad yelled. They dropped their hands to cover themselves.

'George's dad,' shouted George's mum. 'What are you doing? You're stark naked!'

'AHHH!' exclaimed George's dad. 'So are you, George's mum!'

'AHHHHHHHHHHHHHHH!'

Chapter 20

George's parents ran into the shrubs to hide. Neither the running nor the hiding was easily done.

'What's going on?' screamed his mum. 'Why are we so . . . *large*?!'

'I don't know, my head is all foggy!' his dad shouted. 'I can't remember anything, anything at all. Lucy! George!'

'Yes, Dad,' George said stepping out from behind a nearby hedge, making his parents jump.

'What is going on here?' his dad asked.

By now the Council, Maurice, and Karl, and all the hardened criminals had gathered in the garden.

'AHHHHHHHHHH! Who are all these strangers in my garden?' his mum screamed before pointing at Karl. '*What* is that thing?'

'You might need a cup of tea, Mum. And some clothes.'

And so, everyone gathered quickly in the kitchen, and George put the kettle on. George's parents made themselves decent and sat awkwardly opposite the Council and Karl. The large group of hardened criminals stood by, smirking.

'Could someone please explain what is going on here?' asked George's dad.

'Dad, do you remember eating the Spice Bag?'

'George, what's a Spice Bag?'

GASP!

Everyone in the room looked like they were about to have their tonsils inspected.

'What?' asked George's dad looking slightly self-conscious.

'Mum, do you know what a Spice Bag is?'

'A *what*? Is it like a tea bag?'

George explained everything from start to finish, as quickly as he could.

'And then you both turned back into humans, stark naked in the back garden.'

'Well,' said George's dad rather awkwardly. 'Thank you, George, for that, um, detailed narrative.'

Barnaby rose to his feet and the room fell silent, instantly taken by his aura.

'The whole town is in danger,' Barnaby said. 'We shall need to work together, or no one shall be spared.'

'Excuse me,' interrupted George's dad. 'Who are you?'

GASP!

Again, everyone in the room stood, jaws dropped.

'I'm so sorry, Barnaby! He doesn't know . . .'

'George, it's quite alright.'

DING DONG went the doorbell.

Moments later Heidi appeared.

'Heidi, what's the latest at the zoo?'

'Not good, Barnaby. Nearly the entire town is down there. Mr Spicebag and Jasper are preparing thousands of Spice Bags as we speak.'

The room filled with nervous chatter.

'I've got an idea!' called George above all the racket.

But nobody paid George any attention whatsoever.

Lucy let out a loud and piercing whistle.

FWEET!

Everyone fell silent, and Lucy nodded approvingly at George.

'Thank you,' continued George. 'Well, em, my vegetables seem to be the antidote to the Spice Bags. I mean, both my parents ate some and they turned back into people very quickly.'

'But there aren't enough vegetables for the whole town out there!' cried Cry Baby. 'And the supermarkets stopped selling them after Mr Spicebag's opened!'

'Well, I think I have an idea,' George replied. 'But I need everyone to be absolutely quiet.'

The room began to chatter nervously again.

'Silence!' yelled George's dad, slamming his gavel on the kitchen table. 'Now, everyone does what my son says or I will sentence you all to . . . 1,000 days of maths homework!'

The room went deafeningly still. That seemed to do the trick.

A tall criminal's hand went up at the back of the room.

'What is it?' snapped George's dad.

'But I like maths!'

'Then it will be 1,000 days *without* maths homework for you. Have I made myself clear?'

Everyone nodded back at him.

George pushed through the cramped kitchen to the sorry spice rack next to the sink. The small, plastic jars were very dusty indeed. He picked one at random and looked at it closely.

'AHHHH-CHOO!' he sneezed (I told you they were dusty, Reader).

He took each jar from the spice rack and opened every container. He turned to face everybody.

'It's really, *really* important that you all stay very, *veeery* quiet,' whispered George.

Chapter 20

'OK,' said his dad at normal volume.

'SHHHHHHHHHHHHHHHHHHHHHHHHHH-
HHHHH!'

Everyone in the room held an index finger to their lips. George's dad looked apologetic.

George took a bowl from the cupboard and a wooden spoon from the drawer. He inspected the jars. There was nothing special about these spices, but he had to try.

He closed his eyes and took in tiny sniffs as he had been taught.

Curry powder came first and he put it to one side.

Next, garlic powder.

He was unsure whether this was instinct working, or if he was simply smelling the strongest smelling spices. All he had was hope.

A pinch of ground ginger.

A grating of nutmeg.

A shake of tarragon.

On and on and on.

A sprinkle of saffron.

A grind of pepper.

A suspicion of vanilla extract.

He took his time until eventually his gut told him

that he had all he needed. He picked up the wooden spoon, using the handle to crush the spice mix.

Next, he began to mutter softly.

'Please, spices, it's me, George. Mr Spicebag and Jasper are going to turn everyone into animals. I need your help to stop them from taking over the whole town.'

Nothing happened. Not a thing.

But George did not stop.

He crushed and squeezed and squashed. He pressed and pulped and mashed. He milled and powdered and pulverised.

The spices lay limp. Good for nothing but a stew.

'Please, please, *please*, spices,' urged George, beginning to cry. 'This is all my fault. If it wasn't for me Karl would still be himself and Mr Spicebag wouldn't have found the secret recipe. I'm such a fool.'

His voice trembled and he struggled to keep it to a whisper. His tears became more plentiful, his sobs more audible.

'Just help me this one time. Help me and I will never ask for anything ever again. I *promise*.'

Now he couldn't hold back the tears as he desperately ground and crushed the mix. Everyone looked at one another awkwardly. George's mum walked over and rested a kind hand on his shoulder.

'There now, love. You've tried your best, come sit down,' she comforted. George had not heard her speak kindly to him in a long time.

His tears dripped into the spice mix.

DRIP.

DRIP.

DRIP.

And with that, ever so slightly and *eeever* so slowly the spices began to move. George paused his grinding for a moment.

'That's it, spices. Come on.' He muttered some more and he realised that his tears had become the physical manifestation of his desire: to stop Mr Spicebag and Jasper.

The spices began to swirl, gathering pace and power as they spiralled into a tiny twister. Multi-colours flickered wildly and the smells alternated from curry to oregano to five-spice. The mix swirled taller and taller, so much so that George's arm was nearly out of sight.

Suddenly, it hit him. The addictive golly-squash seeds. He had completely forgotten to put them in. Quickly he snatched the seeds from his pocket and dropped them into the bowl. This really fuelled the spices and the twister rose higher and higher. It slammed open all the cupboard doors and all the plates and cups and glasses flew out and *SMASHED* to the floor.

The twister now shone brightly with green and blue colours, blasting cool peppermint air all around the room. Brighter and brighter until ***FLASH!***

CHAPTER
21

The light was blinding. A constant high-pitched ringing rang loudly.

Quickly the room came back into focus. The criminals (now less hardened – soft, if you will) clasped their hands to their ears as they shrieked. George's parents, Lucy, and the Council cowered at the table, their heads in their hands. Maurice and Karl had scarpered into the back garden in terror.

'Hey!' called George above the screaming.

Again, Lucy whistled loudly.

FWEEEEEET!

'It's OK, I think it's stopped,' he said reassuringly.

A wispy cloud floated from the spice mix and a minty fresh smell filled the room. George picked up the bowl and inspected it closely. The spice mix was limp and lame, but he could hear the spices squeak sprightly.

He was unsure what to do. He stepped into the garden with the mix, partly for some peace and quiet, but also because he felt it was the right thing to do. The morning had become much darker and the spits of rain had turned to heavy droplets.

'George, what are you doing out there?' his mum called. 'You'll catch your death. Come back inside.'

George considered the mix thoughtfully. He decided to walk towards his vegetable patch. Again, he could not say why, he just knew that's where he had to be.

'George!' his mum called again, running out after him.

Then everyone spilled out of the kitchen and followed George to the end of the garden. Everyone except his dad, who was too self-important to get wet.

George passed his small greenhouse, his mum in close pursuit, but this time with his raincoat and not to eat him. He reached his vegetable patch and his mum appeared behind him, wrapping the coat around his shoulders.

'What has come over you?' his mum asked gently.

Chapter 21

George ignored her. He ignored everyone.

He stared at the spice mix and knew there was only one thing to be done. He tossed nearly all of it high into the air over his vegetable patch.

George waited for a number of moments but nothing happened. The rain was getting heavier and the mud began to splat.

SPLAT

SPLAT SPLAT

SPLAT SPLAT SPLAT

The group stood by patiently getting wetter and wetter and wetter.

'What's going on here?' one criminal asked another.

'It looks like we're watching the vegetables grow,' answered the other.

'Oh, I see,' considered the first criminal. 'Right, well I suppose I'm up for that cabbage over there.'

'What do you mean?'

'I bet you that cabbage will grow the fastest.'

The second criminal looked at the first criminal like he had two heads.

'Are you mad? Nah, it's got to be that beetroot at the end.'

'*Non*, you are both wrong,' Maurice said. 'Zat caulifleur over zer will win. I can see it in eet's eyes.'

Soon all the criminals were disputing which vegetable would grow the fastest. The row became heated and turned into a mass brawl.

George's dad came charging up the garden having seen the unrest from the kitchen.

'Order! *Order!*' he yelled, very, very slowly jogging past the greenhouse, waving his gavel in his hand.

But it was no use. The rain was falling so heavily that the garden had turned into quite the mud bath, and the criminals were thoroughly enjoying their scuffle.

'I said ORDER!' roared George's dad, appearing at the scene. With that he slipped high into the air, slapping hard on his return to the sludgy ground below.

'OOOOOOOOOOHHHHHHH!' came the prisoners' groans, like a particularly bad choir.

The judge rose slowly to his feet, covered in mud from head to toe. He looked as though he could explode with rage.

But then there came a rumbling sound.

RUMBLE-RUMBLE-RUMBLE

Chapter 21

At first, George thought it must have been his parents'
stomachs, but it was too early for lunch, even for them.

The rumbling grew louder.

RUMBLE-RUMBLE-RUMBLE-RUMBLE

Louder and louder and louder.

RUMBLE-RUMBLE-RUMBLE-RUMBLE-RUMBLE

It felt like an earthquake as the ground shook hard.
George was half expecting the soil to open up and
swallow his house whole.

'Ahhhhhhhhhhhhhh!' cried Cry Baby, pointing at
George's vegetable patch.

George had to rub his eyes to make sure he wasn't
seeing things. His vegetable patch looked as if it was . . .
bobbling.

In actual fact, the vegetables were multiplying. And
fast. One vegetable sprung from another, and another
from that other, and so on. Within thirty seconds, the
amount of vegetables in George's vegetable patch had
quadrupled, and within five minutes the entire back garden
resembled a swimming pool full of . . . well, vegetables.

But it didn't stop there. Oh, no. The vegetables
continued to multiply and soon a pile nearly as high

as the roof sloped against the back of his house and they began to spill out down the side passageways and out onto George's road. It had gotten completely out of hand.

Faster and faster and faster.

Higher and higher and higher the heap of vegetables grew.

'George, do something!' shouted Barnaby. 'We're all going to be crushed if this keeps going.'

George froze, unsure of what to do.

Then he heard screaming. Terrified screaming.

'Lucy!' he yelled, but he could not see his sister anywhere. She was completely covered in vegetables. And now he could feel the vegetables pressing against his legs, then his stomach, then his neck . . . He was about to become completely smothered.

'STOOOOOOOP!' he yelled.

Suddenly, the vegetables did just that. All was still and there wasn't a sound.

For several moments there was silence and then came groans from those buried below.

George pulled himself out and stood atop the mountain of vegetables, which was now as high as the chimneys on his road. By some miracle, nobody was hurt. Lucy, his mum, his dad, the Council, Maurice, Karl and all the softened criminals were all accounted for.

'We've got to get all of these vegetables to the zoo,' George said. 'Mr Spicebag and Jasper have probably turned half the town into animals by now. If the animals eat the vegetables, they'll be turned back into people!'

'You're right, George,' said Barnaby pointedly. 'But how? We must be standing on top of a million vegetables here.'

Nobody spoke as George and the Council considered the best course of action. The criminals played cards, Maurice ate onions, and Karl chewed cabbage leaves. His mum bit her nails, while his dad picked at a particularly difficult mud stain on his tie. Lucy blew bubble gum, which was very annoying – first the sound of the bubble inflating, followed by the inevitable *POP!*

'That's it!' George beamed. 'Hey, Lucy, can you blow another bubble, just like you did before?'

Lucy nodded and blew another pink bubble the size of a large onion.

George walked over to her with the last of the spice mix. He blew the leftovers onto the bubble.

The bubble began to glow.

'Keep going, Lucy! Blow it as big as you can!'

George's phone buzzed. It was Lucy texting him, because she could not talk.

You got it!

Lucy was in her element – texting and blowing bubble gum.

The bubble grew bigger and bigger. It was now double the size of her head. George had to act fast as the bubble was beginning to float. Lucy was now on her tippy toes.

'I need something big enough to carry all of these vegetables!'

'How about the fridge?' suggested his mum.

'It's not big enough!'

George looked around frantically. The bubble was now bigger than Lucy.

'The greenhouse,' shouted Nerd. 'It won't carry all the vegetables, but it will carry a lot!'

'Nerd, you are a genius!' exclaimed George. 'But it's buried under all of this. How are we going to get to it?'

'George, we'll handle this,' yelled Fran, the veteran criminal. 'Come on, you lot, DIG!'

Chapter 21

George had always suspected the other criminals to be somewhat afraid of the little old lady. Now he knew this to be true as immediately all the criminals did as they were told and began to burrow like mice. Maurice nodded approvingly.

'Zey arre vurry good diggerrrs,' the mouse admired, digging into a bulb of garlic.

In no time at all they had managed to burrow right down through the vegetables into the garden below to the greenhouse. Everyone cautiously made their way down so as not to cause an avalanche behind them. Lucy carefully climbed up to the roof of the greenhouse, continuously blowing the bubble bigger and bigger and bigger.

The bubble was soon the size of the greenhouse itself. Nerd tied Lucy to the roof in such a way that she would not float away, while also keeping her body in one piece given the weight she had to carry.

'The marvels of physics,' declared Nerd with a happy sigh, skilfully tying the ropes in place.

'Lucy, keep going,' George called. 'It needs to be bigger if it's to carry all these vegetables.'

The bubble got bigger and bigger. Now it was at least three times the size of the greenhouse which creaked slightly as it began to slowly rise off the ground.

'Quickly, let's get the vegetables in!'

'You heard the boy,' shouted Fran, 'fill her up!'

The criminals did as they were told. Soon it was nearly filled to the brim. George hopped in, up alongside Lucy. The Council and all the criminals held tightly to the greenhouse as it now floated a few feet above ground.

The bubble was now bigger than George's house. It resembled a huge hot air balloon.

'We'll follow you to the zoo,' Barnaby said, as every spare pair of hands held the greenhouse from floating away. 'And George, if you are in trouble you should head towards our treehouse. There will be help there.'

'Wait!' shouted his mum. 'You two are not going anywhere in that death trap without me!'

George's mum squeezed through the gap at the top of the doorway and onto the vegetables next to her children. The greenhouse weighed down a foot or so and Lucy looked like her head might explode with the strain.

'Right, we'll see you soon!' George called as the green-house was about to be released.

'WAAAIT!' yelled George's dad. 'You are not taking *my* greenhouse anywhere without *me*. My greenhouse is the most important thing in the world to me. I'd be lost without my greenhouse. Sure, sometimes my greenhouse annoys me when it talks back to me or when it makes too much noise, but it is my greenhouse and it is my job to make sure it comes back in one piece.'

George could not remember the last time his dad had stepped foot into the garden. He had a feeling that he wasn't talking about the greenhouse at all.

Mr Spicebag

It required at least ten criminals to heave the enormous man inside. The greenhouse planted firmly back down onto the ground with the additional weight.

'Erm, Lucy, a little help!' called George.

The great bubble grew some more and the little greenhouse launched slowly with George and his family inside. Up and up and up into the clouds in the direction of the zoo.

George's phone buzzed.

Did I ever tell you that you are the coolest little brother ever?

CHAPTER
22

The bubble was now about the size of a Third Division football stadium. The dangling greenhouse creaked, groaning slightly with the weight of the vegetables (and George's parents).

Although the bubble was huge, it was also extremely delicate. George was nervous that the smallest collision with the tiniest of birds could send them smashing to the ground.

The weather did not help either. It was a dark morning and the rain battered hard against the glass which made it difficult to hear, but, more importantly, impossible to see.

George's phone buzzed. A text from Lucy.

I can't see anything!

George managed to slide open a window at the side of the greenhouse. The rain instantly swept in, soaking his head from the neck up. But he was able to see much more clearly.

They were very high up indeed. He could just about make out his house and his street far below. On the other side of the town he could make out a red dot which he knew spelt *Mr Spicebag's*. On the outskirts of the town stood the forest and the Council's treehouse. And beyond the forest . . . the zoo.

'Lucy, keep going straight ahead!'

Lucy did well to keep the bubble steady as the weather worsened. Soon the rain turned to hailstones and the noise was ear-splitting. The chance of the bubble bursting was now even greater. George's parents held each other nervously.

The streets below were deserted. No cars, no bikes, no ant-sized people, and George knew why. He had no doubt that word had spread fast about Mr Spicebag's gathering at the zoo.

'Lower, Lucy!'

Lucy slowly released some air from the bubble and they began to descend. They had crossed the town and the tall pines of the forest drifted just below the green-house. George kept a watchful eye out for the zoo.

'As slow as you can, Lucy. We're nearly there.'

They approached the far edge of the forest and sure enough, as the greenhouse turned, he could make out the zoo. Closer and closer, they floated beyond the last of the trees. George now had a clear view of the entrance. To his great surprise, it looked as if there were only a few dozen people down there, but he had a bad feeling.

'Lucy, can you take us over the zoo?'

George's phone buzzed.

Very slowly they floated over the entrance way. The criss-cross cage wrapped around the entire zoo so that no animal, bird or motivated fish could escape.

George was hopeful that Mr Spicebag and Jasper had not caused too much damage. But, alas . . . It was *CHAOS!*

Grown men cried, women shrieked, and children bawled as they transformed into animals or birds or fish.

Mr Spicebag and Jasper stood on top of a massive feeding platform. Mr Spicebag fried and spiced and bagged, while Jasper flung Spice Bag after Spice Bag after Spice Bag into the pit below.

The townspeople were obviously at different stages of transforming – many had already turned into animals, some were mutating, and others pushed and shoved to grab a Spice Bag.

George's mum pointed out various people she knew, and you could tell a small(ish) part of her was quite enjoying it.

Mrs Oates was half human, half donkey. She looked a bit like a centaur – her upper half remaining human for the moment as she donkey-kicked Mrs Samson, the hairdresser, who NEEEEEEIIIIIIIIIGGGGHED in pain before galloping away.

Mr Butler, the bank manager, suddenly sprouted a short, silvery-grey tail. His ears became furry (or, at least, furrier than usual) while his human hands turned into badger paws. Seconds later, he emerged from his suit and shoes, which lay in a heap, and growled at Ms Burke, the local politician, who promptly turned into a snake and sssssssssssssslithered away.

Poor old Mrs Talbot transformed into a rather immobile baboon and was forced to defend herself against Dr Charlton, now a ravenous, wild dog, smacking him on the nose with her walking stick.

Chapter 22

The ridiculously hairy Mr Murphy, George's angry neighbour, turned (perhaps unsurprisingly) into a gorilla, as did his wife. The two seemed perfectly happy grooming one another in the shrubs, nobody daring to approach the two massive beasts.

Mr Parson, the baker, presently a pig, squealed in fear as he scurried away from Thomas, the crocodile, who had always been a crocodile and was delighted with this turn of events.

It was absolute mayhem. On and on and on, the locals morphed and mutated, leaving an array of ripped clothing strewn all around the grounds.

Then came a woman's shrieks.

'Ms Smith!' yelled George.

His favourite, and only, teacher was stuck up a tree while Karl's oafish friends – now hyenas – circled below on their bikes, cackling away. Ms Smith had not eaten any Spice Bags (remember, a vegetarian, Reader) and had remained human this whole time.

'Leave me alone,' Ms Smith cried. 'I don't want any Spice Bags. I just wanted to accompany the children to the zoo to keep them safe. PLEASE!'

The horrible hyenas seemed to take great pleasure

from her fear, and the more she cried, the louder they cackled.

Ms Smith was one of the only nice people in his town – George was not going to let some flea-ridden bullies take her away from him.

'Quick, Lucy. Float us out over the middle of the cage.'

Lucy changed course. By now, there were very few, if any, humans left in the zoo. That is, apart from Mr Spicebag and Jasper who continued to toss Spice Bag after Spice Bag in to the caged animals below.

George waited until they were right above the gorging animals. The drop had to be precise.

'Mum, Dad,' called George as he grabbed hold of the greenhouse door. 'Brace yourselves!'

His parents exchanged worried glances before clutching on to the window frames. George pushed open the glass door and all at once out toppled thousands upon thousands of vegetables, through the criss-cross cage roof and onto the zoo floor.

Carrots and parsnips.

Beetroot and onions.

Cabbages and cauliflowers.

Broccoli and Brussel sprouts.

George and his family waited but nothing happened. Not one animal showed any interest in the vegetables.

'Pathetic!' laughed Mr Spicebag loudly, the sight of the dangling greenhouse and ginormous bubble not throwing him in the slightest.

'They're not interested in the vegetables!' exclaimed George's dad.

'Dad, wait for it . . .'

The animals continued to munch down the Spice Bags. The seagulls ripped through the bags with their beaks. The monkeys carefully extracted the greasy food with their feet. The goats simply ate the entire bag in one go, unconcerned about the paper. The vegetables remained untouched.

But then a bloodhound's head spiked. He sniffed the air and his eyes locked onto the pile of vegetables. He darted from the Spice Bags and began to wolf down the vegetables.

'Oooh, it's the vicar,' said George's mum.

'How can you tell, Mum?'

'His collar.'

Soon the saintly canine was joined by more animals.

Those with the strongest sense of smell were over first, but soon all the animals in the zoo were scoffing the vegetables. Even the Brussel sprouts.

'But I don't understand . . .' said George's dad, scratching his head like a confused bear.

'It's the golly-squash seeds,' George explained. 'They're the ingredient that made everyone in the town obsessed with Spice Bags in the first place.'

'I see,' replied his dad, and for a split second George thought he saw a look of pride on his father's face.

* * *

Gleefully, Mr Spicebag and Jasper continued to fry and spice and fling Spice Bags from the feeding platform into the pit below.

'That's it, Jasper,' Mr Spicebag yelled. 'At this rate we'll be done by teatime!'

Jasper did as he was told but couldn't help notice that many animals had lost interest.

'How very curious.'

Mr Spicebag had just put on a fresh batch and swivelled his skinny neck.

'Very curious *how*?'

'The animals, they're not feeding anymore . . . They're gone. Departed. They've split . . .'

'This isn't right, it's far too fast!'

'What do you mean, Grandad?'

'The transition should take longer. Much longer. They may look like animals, but they need to eat lots and lots and lots if they are to stay animals permanen—' Mr Spicebag stopped short.

'Grandad, what's wrong?'

'SHHH! What's that noise?'

Mr Spicebag and Jasper stood still, silent.

Sure enough, they could make out what sounded like squawking.

'This way!' yelled Mr Spicebag.

Those long legs stormed to the other end of the feeding platform, closely followed by Jasper's significantly shorter legs. From there, they had a clear view of all the commotion.

'NO!' glared Mr Spicebag. 'How is this happening?!'

The sound of the squawking came not from a flock of seagulls, but from a very, very large gathering of very, very embarrassed people. Short people. Tall people.

Skinny people. Fat people. All stark-naked people, shrieking as they ran for cover.

As with George's parents, the vegetables had taken their desired effect, turning the animals back into humans. Except their shoes and shirts and blouses and trousers and skirts had of course been torn to pieces in the morphing process. Thomas, the crocodile (who of course had always been a crocodile), found this all very humorous indeed as he scurried around after his lunch.

'What's going on, Grandad?'

'The vegetables – they're turning them back into humans! How could I have been so *short-sighted*?!' barked Mr Spicebag, scowling up at the greenhouse dangling from the large bubble. His eyes darkened; his bony fists clenched.

Mr Spicebag stormed away.

'What are you going to do?' called Jasper, jogging after him.

'Take back control,' he said through gritted teeth, fuming down the feeding platform.

Quickly, methodically, Mr Spicebag expertly prepared a Spice Bag, dashing the pre-made mix onto the scorching food, the spices squeaking as had become common. He took the finished brown paper bag to the edge of the platform.

'George,' he yelled up at the greenhouse, 'did you really think it would be that easy? You simple, *stupid* boy!'

George's mum had heard enough.

'DO NOT SPEAK TO MY SON LIKE THAT!' she screamed from the greenhouse door. 'HE HAS MORE TALENT IN HIS LITTLE FINGER THAN YOU HAVE IN YOUR ENTIRE BONY BODY!'

George smiled at his mum.

With that, Mr Spicebag tore open the brown paper bag and scoffed the Spice Bag down.

'What's he doing?' asked George's dad.

Mr Spicebag looked angry. Furious. Even from up here George could see those cold, black eyes rage up at him.

First, the sky became even darker. It was only midday yet it looked like it was night-time.

Then the wind picked up even more, sweeping back Mr Spicebag's limp hair – he looked almost bald.

Storm clouds gathered and there came a loud CRASH of thunder in the distance. Lightning *FLASHED* a few seconds later and it began to *pour* rain. I mean really lash down, Reader.

Lucy struggled to keep the bubble in the same position, and they swayed from side to side, the greenhouse dangling perilously.

Then Mr Spicebag's beak-like nose began to bubble and bobble. His long twig fingers glowed green and orange, then blood red. His black, marble eyes began to flame, and his clothes split. Now it was his turn to shudder and shake, and morph and mutate from skin and bones into an alligator, or a snake, or a dinosaur, or an aligatosorus-rex perhaps . . . George couldn't tell. The glow of colours became too bright again but this time, rather than a great flash of light, there came an explosion of flames.

BOOOOOM!

Long, sharp teeth and a jagged, spikey back.

Leathery, veiny wings and fiery red eyes.

A thick, reptilian neck and a powerful serrated tail.

And a piercing screech that would make the hairs on the back of your neck stand up.

Mr Spicebag was no longer man, but dragon. Through a burst of flames, he flew straight for them.

CHAPTER
23

Mr Spicebag let loose another shrill cry. His enormous wings flapped powerfully as he flew up towards them.

Although a giant dragon, Mr Spicebag looked strangely like himself. His teeth were still disgustingly yellow, his claws still bony and oddly twig-like, his frame, although huge, still long and wiry. A film of sweat still matted his brow and he still absolutely stank of Spice Bags. George's parents couldn't help but drool.

The dragon clattered hard into the cage roof, making an extremely large dent.

'He's trapped!' shouted George's mum.

'Not for long,' George yelled. 'Lucy, take us higher. Quickly!'

Lucy did just that, and not a moment too soon as another blast of flames shot up at them from the dragon's blazing mouth, scorching the greenhouse floor beneath them.

Too close, thought George.

The greenhouse floated high above the zoo once more, and sheets of rain swept across the landscape, battering the glass roof.

George again stuck his head out of the window for a better view. Through the rain he could make out the dragon circling inside the cage below, blasting fireball after fireball at the iron enclosure in an attempt to escape.

Mr Spicebag built up more speed and again smashed a further dent into the great cage. *One more ought to do it*, thought George.

It was then that George remembered Barnaby's advice.

'Lucy, take us to the forest. We need to get to the Council's treehouse, there'll be help there.'

'A treehouse?' asked George's mum. 'Shouldn't we call the police? Or the army?'

'Mum, they won't know how to deal with Mr Spicebag. Besides, they're all naked in the zoo!'

'George knows what he's doing,' chimed his dad. 'Onwards and upwards, Lucy.'

Onwards and upwards indeed, into the storm clouds. Now the greenhouse began to shudder violently as thunder BOOMED and lightning *FLASHED*.

Mr Spicebag smashed into the iron cage once more, and this time there was no stopping him. The metal cage sent sparks as it buckled against the dragon's steely skin. Out he escaped, his wings extending full length like a vast pirate ship's sturdy sails.

'Faster, Lucy!' yelled George frantically.

The forest was not far, but the greenhouse was desperately unstable and moved slowly. Mr Spicebag flew up at them with ease. At this rate they had no chance of making it to the Council's treehouse.

But then Lucy, with a stroke of genius, released a blast of air from the bubble and, a bit like a speed boat, they shot across the skyline, the bubble making a very rude sound altogether. George's parents crashed backwards, slamming into the glass walls, and George did not know how much longer the little greenhouse could go on. It hurtled through the air so fast that it was impossible to see where they were going, and this time George could not simply stick his head out of the window for risk of hitting an ill-fated pigeon.

Mr Spicebag let out another piercing screech, almost mocking them. He flew alongside the speeding greenhouse which looked even more delicate by comparison. He was so close that his fiery, slit pupils stared in through the glass.

'Did you really think you would beat me, George?' Mr Spicebag sneered.

The greenhouse continued at a fierce speed and reached the forest in record time. Mr Spicebag spun playfully alongside them, smashing high flying trees with his thorny back and jagged tail. He spat fire as he glided, mainly for the fun of it but partly to show off, leaving a trail of destruction below as the old church steeple burned and some ancient oak trees smouldered.

'How shall I finish you, hmmm?' toyed Mr Spicebag. 'Maybe I could pop this bubble with one of my talons? Or scorch you into smithereens? Or perhaps I could smash the lot of you with my jagged tail? I'll tell you what, how about I let your parents decide, George? After all, they *are* my best customers.'

The blood drained from George's face. There was no coming back. No great escape. They were doomed.

George's life flashed before his eyes. His first steps. His first gardening kit. His first pickle and onion sandwich (he did not like it).

Then through all the wind and the rain, and Mr Spicebag's shrill laughter, there came a dull sound that was barely audible. But it was powerful and it prevailed.

The rain continued to lash and the wind continued to howl, but the dragon's laughter stopped.

'What's that *noise?*' Mr Spicebag snapped, peering down into the dark forest below.

As the sound grew louder, George knew exactly what it was. It was unique and one he could never forget. The Council's horn was summoning them to safety.

'*Where* is that coming from?' Mr Spicebag roared, the noise irritating his sensitive ears immensely.

The dragon circled low above the forest to investigate. It was pitch black down there. That is, until a single, solitary light flickered from the ground. A candle. It was like spotting a star in the night sky, for once one appeared, suddenly there were two, then three, then a dozen flickered and so on. Soon George could make out hundreds of candles down there.

The horn continued to sound and Mr Spicebag flew right down towards the heart of the forest. The enormous dragon dwarfed the Council's treehouse which sat high atop the great Copper Beech. And at the top of the treehouse stood a recognisable, lone figure. Barnaby. The Council leader glared up at the flying, greasy beast, blowing determinedly into the horn. Mr Spicebag locked eyes onto the 90-year-old-looking boy.

'Stop that racket, old man!' he rasped, but Barnaby ignored him.

The dragon let out a furious blast of flames and flew straight for the treehouse.

'NOW, CRY BABY!' yelled Barnaby suddenly.

Out from the base of the tree stepped Cry Baby. The dragon grinned widely and swept down at the teary-eyed boy.

Then Cry Baby began to scream, not through fear but in strategy. The screaming grew louder and louder, and so incredibly high pitched that George could see the greenhouse glass crack some more. Mr Spicebag roared in pain, upturning quickly.

Cry Baby ran out of breath and looked exhausted. The Council's horn sounded once more.

'Lower, Lucy,' yelled George. 'Quick, we've got to get down.'

The clearing at the heart of the forest now resembled an airport runway, such was the vast number of candles. The greenhouse dipped lower and was just a stone's throw above the Council's treehouse, but there was not enough time. Without Cry Baby's screaming, the dragon regained focus. Mr Spicebag was raging, his slit pupils flaming, and he began to torch trees all around him.

Screaming could be heard from the ground below, and through all the chaos, George could not help but think back to the vase which he had broken in Mr Spicebag's chipper depicting the dragon's attack on the tribal town. The beautiful drawings seemed almost like a prophecy.

George's daydream was short-lived as a fireball narrowly missed the greenhouse from above and his parents shrieked loudly. What looked like a flaming arrow then flew directly up at Mr Spicebag's eyes from the ground below. Then another. And another. Then a frenzied attack. But they weren't arrows – it was flaming wax.

Dozens of children stood at the edge of the forest, firing candles of all shapes and sizes. The burning wax flew into the dragon's eyes, blinding Mr Spicebag, if only temporarily. He let out the most horrendous of shrieks, flailing through the air as his eyes were scorched.

A sharp whistle cut through the air and George recognised Sweets below. He walked purposefully out into the clearing towards the dragon. Without any fuss, he began to fire large rocks at Mr Spicebag with an impressive-looking sling-shot, and the other children followed his lead.

'Those rocks aren't nearly big enough,' remarked George's dad.

In fact, they were not rocks at all, but hard candy. *Very* hard candy. Candy that would cause your teeth to rot just by looking at it.

'They're aiming for his teeth!' shouted George with a smile.

The bombardment of hard candies continued, chipping away at Mr Spicebag's horrible teeth cavity by cavity. But the dragon was too powerful, and sent flames smashing to the ground. Sweets and his followers retreated quickly into the forest as the ground was incinerated behind them.

Next, there appeared large wooden structures from the other side of the dark forest.

'What are those?' asked George's mum.

'Are they . . . catapults?' replied his dad, taking out his spectacles.

Nerd waved the tall wooden machines forward: six gigantic catapults, each being loaded up with ammunition.

'More sweets?' asked George's dad.

'Conkers,' smiled George.

'Conkers?' asked his mum.

'They store tonnes of conkers away every year. Now I know why!'

At Nerd's signal, the great wooden devices each flipped thousands of conkers through the air. The design was flawless; the conkers flew like bullets. While many simply bounced off the dragon's rugged skin, others shot inside Mr Spicebag's eyes, ears, mouth, and nostrils.

'They're trying to pick off Mr Spicebag's senses one by one!' George said and clapped.

Chapter 23

The attack continued for several minutes. Hard candies from one side, conkers from the other, and the flaming candle assault straight at Mr Spicebag's eyes.

Then came the pots and pans led by Addy, galloping forward on top of Karl. Hundreds and hundreds of roaring children spilled into the heart of the forest thudding, whacking, slamming, smashing, and screaming so that the dragon went wild with the noise, flames being fired here, there, and everywhere.

The courageous army of children continued, and efforts were made to tie up Mr Spicebag. Arrows shot up and over and under the dragon from all angles, this time carrying ropes, string, shoelaces, and old cords all knotted together. Again and again, the arrows flew, and bit by bit the dragon tired. Somehow, rather incredibly, the children seemed to have overcome Mr Spicebag, who became entangled and breathed wearily before collapsing in a heap.

The children cheered triumphantly, but George felt something was amiss.

Although Mr Spicebag looked completely entwined, he suddenly began to laugh, fire snorting from his nostrils. Then without any trouble at all, the dragon broke free, standing upright. Undoing all their good work, he outstretched his veiny wings wide, as if he was flexing his muscles.

'Futile! You will NEVER beat me!'

It had been a trap! He had tricked the children to get them into the heart of the forest so that he'd have more targets. Fireball after fireball scorched the ground below as the children scarpered in panic.

'George, I have an idea.'

'What is it, Dad?'

'There's no time to explain. But I need you to do what I say and trust what I do.'

George stalled before nodding his agreement.

'Promise me, George. I want to hear you say it.'

'OK, I promise!'

George's dad walked over to the greenhouse door and looked out at Mr Spicebag, who was now scorching the Council's treehouse.

'*FWEEEEEEEEEEEEEEET!*' whistled George's dad loudly.

Mr Spicebag bombed towards the greenhouse, a look of destruction in his eyes.

'WAAAAAIT!' yelled George's dad.

Chapter 23

Mr Spicebag halted in his stride, considering George's dad.

'I've decided you can eat me. But *only* me!'

'Only you?' sneered Mr Spicebag. 'That's not part of the arrangement.'

'Well, I'll be more than enough. Look at me!'

The dragon laughed heartily.

'You have a sense of humour, I'll give you that!' said the dragon, not entirely convinced.

'I'll tell you what, start with me and see how you feel!'

The dragon deliberated.

'You've got yourself a deal, Mr George's dad!'

George's dad shook one of Mr Spicebag's talons to seal the deal.

'Dad, seriously. What's the plan, here?'

'Plan?' asked George's dad.

'Yes!' said George, an urgency in his voice. 'Plan!' George's dad calmly closed the greenhouse door and faced his son.

'Well, the plan is that I let Mr Spicebag eat me . . .'

'No!' cried George.

'Yes,' continued his dad, 'and on my way down his throat, I'll be the most irritating and distracting crumb he'll have ever eaten. Now, you and your mum and Lucy will need to get to the ground as quickly as possible and escape into the forest.'

'NO, Dad!'

'Yes!' his dad said firmly, grabbing his son by the shoulders. 'You promised me, George!'

'You can't do this, Dad!' wept George.

His dad hunched down and pulled his son in close for a great, big bear hug. George had forgotten how nice this felt.

'Look at me, George,' he said softly, and George looked up reluctantly. 'You and your sister have done so well. I'm so proud. You will always be my little bear.'

George's dad embraced his son tenderly one last time. He tucked in his shirt for some reason and pulled up his belt well above his very generously sized belly. He tied his shoelaces and adjusted his tie, and when there was nothing left to be done, he stepped forward and opened the greenhouse door.

'I'm ready!' shouted George's dad.

Mr Spicebag laughed some more.

'Oh, goody!' he mocked. 'I'm starved!'

The enormous dragon circled around the greenhouse before dipping beneath and approaching from below. His jaw opened wide and George's dad stared down into the deep throat and at those countless sharp, yellow teeth. He took one last glance at his family and faced Mr Spicebag.

But before his dad could jump, George broke free from his mum and dived like a cannonball, straight down Mr Spicebag's throat.

CHAPTER
24

Without ceremony, the dragon swallowed George whole.

GULP!

'Mm-mmm, delicious!' exclaimed Mr Spicebag, rubbing his gob with a scaly claw. Although dragon, he was still almost human in his manner.

'Who would have thought that a 10-year-old boy would be so tasty,' he continued. 'A little underdone, perhaps, but I'll make sure to cook my main course.'

'You monster!' wailed George's mum, falling to her knees.

George's parents sobbed into each other's arms. The bubble deflated as Lucy too joined them in tears. The greenhouse dropped gently into the heart of the forest,

Chapter 24

which was now very muddy, and flamed and smoked like a real battlefield.

'Oh, don't cry!' mocked Mr Spicebag. 'You should be proud. Your boy was *so* delicious.'

The fresh meat gave the dragon a new-found energy, and with an almighty blast of flames he scorched the Council's treehouse completely.

'Don't you all see!' rasped Mr Spicebag loudly, the treehouse blazing fiercely. '*This* is what happens when you fight back! You will quickly learn that there is a new order, that I am top of the food chain, and that I AM KING!'

The dragon shrieked ominously, a deathly shrill piercing the air. His screeches were almost a declaration of triumph.

Storm clouds grew heavy and distant thunder rumbled once more. The only light now came from the flaming treehouse, which represented the end of the old and the start of the new regime.

But as the flames engulfed the treehouse, the dragon's triumphant laughter strangely stopped. Mr Spicebag growled, as if in discomfort, like he had indigestion or heart burn. Then his steely chest began to glow . . .

Mr Spicebag

At first the light was so faint that, were it not for the miserable day, you probably would have missed it altogether. But then it shone brighter and brighter. So brightly, in fact, that you could not look directly at it, even with sunglasses.

The light must have been hot too as the dragon began to shriek with pain, as if being branded with a thousand cattle irons. He contorted backwards in agony, his great veiny wings twisting rearward, his blinding bright chest pressing upwards.

Suddenly a fork of light flashed from the dragon's chest, and for the second time in a few hours Mr Spicebag began to shudder and shake, and morph and mutate. His huge wings went up in flames and for a moment it looked as if he would be engulfed entirely. But then a skinny, skeletal arm came into view, and two long pins for legs, and his horrible grease-smeared face appeared.

He got smaller and smaller, shrinking at speed. His body glowed fiery red and yellow, then orange, purple, green, and finally brown and grey and black.

And of course, without wings, Mr Spicebag couldn't stay airborne. He dropped from the sky fast – and faster, and *faster*. And the closer he came to hitting the ground, the more he returned to his former self. All except for his belly, that is, which stayed inflated – as if something or someone were stuck inside.

As the rest of his body continued to shrink back to normal, his stomach began to stretch and stretch and stretch. Mr Spicebag began to yell and scream – there was no way that his belly could hold much longer!

SPLAT!

For several moments, no one could see through the smoke. There was an almighty stench of spice in the air. It really did look like a battlefield now as a thick fog lingered above the sludgy field.

George's dad waded through the thick mud, waving away the mist in front of him. Bits of Mr Spicebag had splattered everywhere. A bony arm and a beaked nose here. A yellow tooth and a sweaty eyebrow there. And his floppy bow tie still intact. The wiry tyrant had been quite thoroughly extinguished.

Then, as the air cleared, a small, scrawny figure emerged.

'George!' cried his dad.

All present watched on as George's parents waded through the mud, slipping and sliding as they did, before embracing their favourite, and only, son.

The cheers were rapturous. The whistles and cries joyous.

'What were you thinking?' cried George's mum, kissing her son's cheeks repeatedly.

'Turnip seeds,' George replied with a grin.

'Turnip seeds?' Lucy asked.

'I knew that my vegetables would turn Mr Spicebag back to himself, but we had none left in the greenhouse. Then I remembered I still had some turnip seeds in my pocket that Ms Smith gave me,' explained George, producing the small packet of seeds.

'You brilliant, disobedient little genius!' beamed George's dad, hugging him tightly.

'Did I tell you that you are the coolest little brother ever?' Lucy said and smiled, wrapping an arm around his shoulder.

'Yes,' grinned George.

A celebratory mood overcame the battlefield despite the damage done. The fog lifted and the forest was showered with sunshine, as if a spell had been broken.

Chapter 24

The Council gathered around George to give him a well-earned pat on the back, even Wax. All beamed widely, except for their great leader.

'George,' called Barnaby anxiously. 'What about Jasper?'

Throughout all this terrifying excitement, George had completely forgotten about that two-faced traitor.

'You're right, Barnaby!'

Without delay, George tore off towards the zoo. He ran slowly, however, such was his athletic ability. Mercifully, Karl – who had not yet been turned back to his former self – scooped George up so that our hero landed firmly on the giant lizard's back. Off they galloped, with George's family, the Council, and hundreds of children clanging their pots and pans in pursuit.

George completely underestimated the intimidating lizard's staggering speed, and they made it to the zoo in record time. After a quick vomit in a nearby dustbin, George rode atop Karl in through the entrance and into the cage where more chaos awaited.

Jasper stood on the platform high above, flinging Spice Bag after Spice Bag into the pit below. Although all the vegetables had been eaten, he had managed to undo a lot of George's good work as the greedy townspeople could not resist the Spice Bags. Many of them had actually turned back into animals!

'Jasper!' yelled George.

George's former friend grinned cruelly at our dragon slayer.

'Your grandad, Jasper,' called George. 'I'm sorry but . . . he's gone!'

Jasper stopped what he was doing.

'Gone? What do you mean?!'

'He ate some turnip seeds and exploded!'

For a moment, Jasper stood speechless.

'He's . . . *gone*?' called Jasper again, but he did not look sad or alarmed or surprised.

In fact, he looked . . . happy. Delighted. Thrilled.

'Jasper, just give up!'

'Don't you see, Georgie!' beamed Jasper. 'This means that I will be in charge!'

Jasper picked up a Spice Bag and tore it open.

'The power will be all mine!' Jasper shouted, dangling a handful of the food above his mouth. 'The King is dead . . . Long live the King!'

Quick as a flash, Karl bolted from George through

the chaotic Spice Bag eating frenzy. George had never seen anything move so fast, not on the nature programmes on TV or the cheetahs in the pit a safe distance away.

The huge lizard's legs pounded so fast that, in little more than a heartbeat, he was on the feeding platform just a few paces from Jasper. The devious boy was shocked at the sight of Karl, but quickly stuffed the Spice Bag into his mouth. Now that he knew the antidote, the unhinged boy had no difficulty changing into an animal.

The transformation was abrupt. With a *CRACK* like a whip and a *FLASH* of light, the unfaithful boy – now an impressive falcon – took flight. He had razor-sharp talons and a strong, curved beak with sharp edges to cut up his dinner. He had pale, yellow eyes with binocular vision, and his wings were long and narrow. Round and round, Jasper soared with perfect precision.

'Don't you see,' cried Jasper in his now cawing voice. 'I am in charge! There will be no escaping my control. You, Georgie, are vermin, and we all know what happens to vermin!'

Talons at the ready, the falcon swooped at George. Unfortunately for Jasper, however, he had not considered the length of Karl's tongue, which could easily reach the length of a small swimming pool. The giant lizard had run out of platform but snapped out his tongue like a fishing rod. Without any trouble at all, he reefed the nasty bird of prey from the air and down into his sizeable gorge, leaving nothing but a few falcon feathers to mop up.

'BUUUUUUUUUUUUUUUUUUUUUUUUUUU
UUUUUUUUUUURRRPP!'

Karl's belch was like music to George's ears.

Chapter 24

And that *really* did it. This time, I promise you, Reader, George (with some help, of course) had saved his town from the greasy grasp of the Spice Bag.

* * *

As I've said, this story has a beginning, a middle, and an end. I always prefer to finish at the end.

The locals were all turned back into people with the vast number of vegetables in George's back garden. Well, most of them were turned back. The ridiculously hairy Mr Murphy, George's neighbour, was quite happy to remain a gorilla. Although a very, very hairy man, he was only an averagely hairy gorilla and enjoyed poking fun at the ridiculously hairy gorillas at the zoo.

Mr Benson, George's headmaster, upheld his end of the bet. To this day, he wears a wedding dress to work, which he finds liberating in more ways than one.

Ms Smith continued being a kind and enthusiastic teacher who often got her facts wrong. In years to come she would retell this story many, many times, but in her version, George was a dog. Or was it a trout?

Maurice, the hungry French mouse, moved in with George's family. He likes to sing in the shower.

Karl was turned back to his former self, and he and his mother won the mother–son tap dancing competition for the third year running. George and Karl felt it appropriate in the circumstances, and for the good of this story, to become best friends.

Barnaby entered secondary school and, therefore, to everyone's dismay, was forced to resign from the Council of the Elder Children. Wax took over as leader. He did not make George an Elder Child.

Things really looked up for George though. For one, the town as a whole decided, really rather reluctantly, that their obsession with Spice Bags was unhealthy and closed down Mr Spicebag's chipper. The supermarkets and the grocers began to sell vegetables again. And who was their supplier? That's right! Because no one else knew how to grow vegetables anymore, George made an absolute fortune as the sole supplier of vegetables in town. With all this money, he could do whatever he pleased, which was anything at all, so long as he was with his family.

Lucy began to give flying lessons. Her bubble-flying technique was considered by some to be astonishingly

Chapter 24

risky and, as one newspaper described it, 'a lawsuit waiting to happen'. However, most decided that it was better for the environment than planes, and they boycotted that newspaper, putting it out of business. Aeroplanes soon went out of fashion and people only flew by bubble gum. In years to come, Lucy would set up Bubble Gum Airlines, provider of the cheapest form of air travel: a user-friendly piece of bubble gum, allowing people to chew, blow and float to wherever they liked, whenever they pleased.

George's dad continued to be a judge, which of course still involved his shouting at hardened criminals, but this time from the treadmill, and he always made time to give George great big bear hugs and tell him stories about penguins flying aeroplanes or horses pretending to be zebras to get into Z-rated films. George's mum liked to fuss over her son again too, and would tuck him into bed at night so tightly that he knew he was safe from rolling onto the (pretend) burning lava floor beneath

George's town was now a glorious one. It was almost always sunny but there was more to it than that. As he walked past the local playground, the children played.

As he passed by the shops and restaurants, the lights shone bright. And as he passed by the salad bar, the queues were long and chatty because now salad bars actually existed. In fact, the only light that he could not see was the red fluorescent writing that used to read 'Mr Spicebag's'.

Acknowledgements

I wish to thank all at HarperCollins, in particular my publisher, Conor Nagle, for his great belief in the book, my editors, Nora Mahony and Catherine Gough, for their fantastic wisdom and support, and the cover designer, Graham Thew; my copy-editor, Síne Quinn, and my proofreader, Emma Dunne, for their eagle eyes; my supremely talented illustrator, Helen O'Higgins, for helping to bring the characters to life; my friend and confidant, Robert Crowley, for his wise ears and constructive feedback; my family for their endless support.

Most of all, I would like to thank my utterly magnificent wife, Zelda, for your love and constant encouragement, and my son, Rafe, for being the most precious alarm clock I could ask for.